"Thanks for coming to my rescue."

Rachel's voice was warm with gratitude. Impulsively she moved closer to Richard. "I don't know what I would have done without you."

"I think," Richard said slowly, "I'm entitled to a little more than a mere thank you. I noticed the other day at Eilean Dorcha that you were being quite friendly toward Ben Carson. What's good enough for him can't be bad for me."

Swiftly he caught her to him, almost crushing her with the strength of his arms as his mouth came down on hers. For a moment she was powerless to move, then the implication of his words hit her.

Furiously she brought up her hand and gave him a stinging blow on the cheek. "How dare you!" she raged.

WELCOME
TO THE WONDERFUL WORLD
OF *Harlequin Romances*

Interesting, informative and entertaining,
each Harlequin Romance portrays an appealing
and original love story. With a varied array
of settings, we may lure you on an African safari,
to a quaint Welsh village or an exotic Riviera
location—anywhere and everywhere that adventurous
men and women fall in love.

As publishers of Harlequin Romances, we're
extremely proud of our books. Since 1949,
Harlequin Enterprises has built its publishing
reputation on the solid base of quality and
originality. Our stories are the most popular
paperback romances sold in North America; every
month, six new titles are released and sold at
nearly every book-selling store in Canada and the
United States.

A free catalogue listing all available Harlequin Romances
can be yours by writing to the

HARLEQUIN READER SERVICE,
(In the U.S.) M.P.O. Box 707, Niagara Falls, N.Y. 14302
(In Canada) Stratford, Ontario, Canada N5A 6W2

or use coupon at back of book.

We sincerely hope you enjoy reading
this Harlequin Romance.

Yours truly,

THE PUBLISHERS
  Harlequin Romances

Shadow
of Celia

by

ELIZABETH JEFFREY

Harlequin Books

TORONTO • LONDON • NEW YORK • AMSTERDAM
SYDNEY • HAMBURG • PARIS

Original hardcover edition published in 1979
by Mills & Boon Limited

ISBN 0-373-02271-9

Harlequin edition published July 1979

Printed in U.S.A.

CHAPTER ONE

IT was still raining when the boat docked at Dunglevin. Cars and people began spilling off, so Rachel Canfield picked up her suitcase, put up her umbrella and followed the crowd. With her blonde hair hanging straight and shining to her shoulders she was a slightly taller-than-average girl, trim-figured in a navy trouser suit and brightly coloured blouse. Attractive without being pretty, her bone structure was good but her nose was just a shade too long and her mouth just a shade too wide for beauty. Her eyes, though, were quite lovely, large and a deep violet. On close inspection, however, they held a look of suffering that went far beyond her twenty-four years.

'The buses for Glencarrick?' she enquired of the man who took her ticket. He was thick-set, with receding grey hair and bad feet.

'Twice a week. Tuesdays and Fridays.'

'But this is Wednesday!' Rachel's heart sank to her knees.

The man shrugged.

'How far is it, then? Can I walk?'

He looked down at her platform shoes and his expression was eloquent.

'Ye might. In aboot three days. Glencarrick's thirty miles from here.'

'Oh.' Rachel's heart sank from her knees to the ground. She pushed a strand of damp hair away from her face. This was all she needed! She turned away with a sigh. She had never wanted to come to Scotland

in the first place, but her father had insisted on writing
to his sister—whom Rachel had never met—telling her
of Keith's tragic death and Rachel's subsequent break-
down and suggesting that a change of scenery might be
helpful. Her aunt's reply had been prompt and welcom-
ing, but it was more to please her parents than anything
that Rachel had agreed to the visit. Now that she no
longer had Keith it made little difference to her where
she was or what she did. Life had lost all meaning for
her six months ago. She began to walk along the pier
towards the road, hardly aware of what she was doing,
her mind back on that terrible evening when they had
come to tell her that Keith, the young solicitor she was
to have married in less than a month, had been killed
when his plane crashed on the way home from a business trip to Germany. Even now, desolation swept over
her as she remembered that night, and the tears—after
all these months still never very far from the surface—
welled up in her eyes.

'Are you the young lady who's anxious to get to
Glencarrick?'

Rachel looked up mistily and was aware of a tall
man in his early thirties, with a deep, pleasant voice
which altered impatiently as he said, 'Oh, heavens,
you're surely not weeping because there isn't a bus!'

She sniffed and pulled herself together. 'Certainly
not,' she said icily. 'A piece of grit got in my eye, if you
must know. I was just about to call a taxi, although
I can't see that it's any business of yours.' She turned
her back and bent to pick up her suitcase.

It was taken from her grasp. 'There's no need. I'm
going that way myself, I'll give you a lift. Kilfinan
Cottage?'

Rachel looked at him in amazement. 'How did you
know that?'

'The Glen is sparsely populated, so news spreads pretty quickly. You'll be Rose's niece.' It was a statement, not a question, so Rachel decided it didn't need an answer. Relieved to have transport, although she didn't care much for the man himself, she followed him to the Range Rover parked nearby and waited while he stowed her suitcase, then she climbed in beside him, stealing a glance at his profile as she did so. He wasn't exactly good-looking; striking would be a more accurate description. His face was long, his nose slightly aquiline, his jaw firm to the point of sternness. His eyes, behind the heavy glasses he wore for driving, were deep-set and very dark. In fact everything about him was dark; his hair was thick, slightly curling and jet black, he wore a black roll-neck sweater, even his skin was dark—brown and weatherbeaten. He looked lean and athletic, as if most of his time was spent out of doors and his hands on the steering wheel were strong, square, and capable. He handled the Range Rover with complete assurance.

They drove in silence out of the town and along narrow roads that curled their way between mountains that looked like gigantic black bonfires where the rain-clouds smouldered over them. Clutches of soggy sheep grouped spasmodically along the way watched balefully as they passed.

'It doesn't always rain like this,' he volunteered at last, 'although I must admit that we do get more than our fair share in these parts.'

'It makes no difference to me what the weather is like.' Rachel was tired after the journey, but even so she hadn't intended to let her voice sound quite so flat.

He turned his head and his eyes met hers. They were totally unsympathetic. 'Yes, we've heard about your unfortunate affair. I'm sorry. But these things happen, you know; you can't live in the past.' He turned his attention back to the road, which was now climbing steeply by the side of a loch.

Rachel opened her mouth to reply, but no words would come. Who was this man? What right had he to speak to her in such a callous manner? And how was it that he knew so much about her? Was Aunt Rose, about whom she knew so little, nothing more than a gossipy old woman who couldn't keep her affairs to herself? Rachel frowned. She knew nothing about her father's sister, except that she was unmarried and had kept house for Alistair Duncan, an elderly man who lived at Kilfinan House, for the past thirty years. Suddenly Rachel realised what a fool she had been. It was only to please her father that she had agreed to visit this aunt; now here she was, in a godforsaken spot miles from anywhere, where the rain fell in relentless icy needles and where, it would seem, you couldn't call your soul your own. She had come all this distance to try and forget what had happened—how her life, so full of hope and promise, had been so suddenly and cruelly shattered. Instead of which, the first person she met knew of her tragedy and wasted no time in reminding her of it. Clearly, it had been a mistake ever to have come here.

Seething inside, she turned to him. 'Would you stop the car, please.' It was not too late. She could stay in an hotel in Dunglevin tonight and return to her home in Suffolk tomorrow.

The road was still climbing upwards. It appeared to have been carved out of the side of the mountain which rose, steep and craggy to one side, while on the other side it fell away to the loch below, guarded, but only where the road bent sharply or the drop was precipitous, by a crash barrier.

Since the man beside her appeared not to have heard, Rachel repeated her question.

'I heard you the first time, but don't you realise that you can't stop willy-nilly on roads like these? You'll have to wait until we come to a passing place,' he replied shortly. 'There's one a little way ahead. Ah, here we are.' He pulled into a fairly wide parking area, built out over a natural bulge in the mountainside and parked, it seemed to Rachel, who had no head for heights, precariously near to the edge. The rain still drummed unmercifully on the roof of the car and ran in rivulets down the windscreen, too fast for the wipers to cope with. Her companion leaned on the steering wheel and gazed at her. 'Well, what are you intending to do, get out and walk?' he asked. 'Before you do, perhaps you should know that we're well over half way to Glencarrick now, so you've a long trek back to Dunglevin. It's a bit damp out there, too, and you're not really dressed for it. Still, it's up to you—and if you do get out and walk spare a glance for the view, it's one of the finest in these parts. But make up your mind, because I want my tea.' He spoke in a completely matter-of-fact tone that infuriated Rachel even further.

Savagely, she pushed open the car door, but the force of the wind and rain blew it shut again before she had a chance to get out.

'I thought you'd see sense.' Before she had time to open it again the man beside her had let up the clutch and the car had begun to move again. Humiliated, Rachel huddled in her seat, not speaking, for the rest of the journey, which took them down the mountain road, through the little fishing town at its foot and then inland to Glencarrick, where the clachan, or village, nestled in a hollow and Kilfinan House, sitting squarely on the lower slopes of the mountainside, commanded a view of the entire glen. In spite of the rain, in spite of her unprepossessing introduction to the area, indeed, in spite of herself, Rachel couldn't help being impressed by the sight of the big white house set among the trees.

At the lodge gates the man stopped the car. 'This is your destination,' he said, getting out and reaching for her suitcase. 'No doubt Rose will have the kettle on.'

Rachel doubted if he heard her grudging words of thanks as he climbed back into the Range Rover and drove off down the glen. She still had no idea who he was, and she didn't much care. She simply hoped she wouldn't see him again.

Aunt Rose greeted her cordially enough, although she was obviously surprised to see her. Rachel could see no family likeness in her aunt; she was a tiny woman, very thin, her face sallow and lined. And it didn't help her rather stern appearance that she wore her hair, dark and streaked with grey, dragged back into an uncompromising knot.

'How did you get here? There are no buses,' Her aunt's voice was unexpectedly low and well-modulated. 'I'd arranged for Ben to meet you in Dunglevin to-morrow. I wasn't expecting you until the twenty-second, you see.'

'But this *is* the twenty-second,' Rachel said, adding uncertainly, 'isn't it?'

'No, tomorrow's the twenty-second.' Rose patted her arm. 'But no matter, my girl, you're here now and I'm pleased to see you. Someone gave you a lift?'

'Yes.' Rachel didn't elaborate on her rather uncomfortable encounter.

Rose nodded. 'People are very good in that way around here. Now, draw up to the fire while I set the table. Oh, this is Melanie, by the way, Mr Duncan's granddaughter. She spends quite a lot of time here with me when she's not roaming with Ben.' Rose nodded towards the corner, where a little girl of about six was curled in an armchair. She was a pretty child, or would have been had it not been for the strange, almost hunted look that she wore. She had thick black hair, cut in a low fringe, and pale, elfin face. She was staring into the fire with enormous brown eyes, apparently oblivious of Rachel's entrance.

'Hullo, Melanie,' Rachel said with a smile, but the child paid no attention and continued staring into the fire.

'She won't talk to you. She doesn't talk to anyone,' Aunt Rose explained. 'Take no notice.' She was busy laying the table with home-made scones and oatcakes as she spoke.

Rachel warmed herself gratefully at the fire. Despite the fact that it was late June the rain had chilled her to the bone and she felt herself shivering, mainly with cold but partly with apprehension. Her welcome to Scotland had not been altogether overwhelming, so far.

As she warmed herself she could feel Melanie's eyes on her and with a smile she turned to look at the child. Immediately, the big brown eyes were averted and the child seemed to shrink back even further into the corner of the armchair.

'She needs the company of other children. She's alone too much,' Rose said, pouring out tea.

'Doesn't she meet other children at school?'

'She doesn't go to school. They tried her at the local school, but it didn't work; in fact, it made her worse than ever. Her father wants to send her away to school, but Mr Duncan wants to have a governess for her. He says she's had enough upheavals in her life without adding more. He's right, too.'

Rachel was puzzled. Her aunt was talking in riddles. Talking about Melanie, too, as if the child wasn't present.

'Come along, Melanie. On your chair,' said Rose.

Obediently, the little girl slid from her armchair to her chair at the table and began to eat the scone that Rose had placed before her. At least, Rachel reflected, there was nothing wrong with the child's hearing.

Gratefully, Rachel drank two cups of tea and sampled her aunt's delicious baking while she gave the older woman news of her family.

Aunt Rose sighed. 'I would like to have seen Frank again....'

Frank was Rachel's father. 'Why don't you come and spend a holiday with Dad and Mother?' asked Rachel. 'I know they'd love to see you.'

Rose shrugged. 'Maybe one day....' her voice trailed off.

Suddenly Melanie slid off her chair and ran to the window, her face, for the first time since Rachel arrived, animated. There was the sound of a car door slamming.

'Oh, that'll be Ben. You always hear him coming, don't you child? Well, come along then, fetch your anorak. You don't want to keep him waiting, do you?' Rose spoke brusquely but not unkindly to Melanie.

Melanie went for her anorak as the door opened and a young man entered. He was very tall with craggy features and brown curly hair. His eyes were blue and had deep laughter lines at the corners, giving him a good-natured appearance. He stood filling the doorway, rain glistening on his hair, his hands thrust deep in the pockets of his rather-the-worse-for-wear parka.

'Ben,' Aunt Rose said briefly, by way of introduction. 'Manages the Estate for Mr Duncan. My niece Rachel, here for a holiday.' Rachel gained the impression that Rose didn't care much for this big shaggy man, although he seemed pleasant enough as far as Rachel could tell.

Ben returned her greeting and then turned to Melanie, who had flung herself at him, picking her up and letting her burrow into his shoulder.

'Time to go home, poppet. Your daddy's waiting for you.' He spoke with only the merest trace of a Scottish burr.

Melanie shook her head fiercely, but she was grinning. Obviously this was a game they often played. 'Say goodbye and thank you to Rose,' Ben instructed, putting her down.

The little girl went over to Rose, stood in front of her and gave a stiff, unsmiling nod. Then she flung herself back at Ben.

Turning to leave, Ben said to Rachel, 'Goodbye now. If you'd care to come with me tomorrow I'll show you round the Estate.' At this Melanie beat him on the chest with her fists, pointing to herself in between. 'We'll see, poppet,' he smiled, 'maybe if you're very good you can come too.' He looked at Rachel again. 'The sun will be shining tomorrow.' With a smile of farewell he left, taking the strange little girl with him.

'What's wrong with Melanie?' Rachel asked her aunt as she helped with the washing up.

Rose shrugged. 'Nobody seems to know. She simply won't talk. She's been to specialists in Edinburgh and they say there's no physical reason for it; her hearing's normal and there's no sign of any defect in her palate. She simply doesn't talk.'

'She's always been like this?'

'It's been worse since her mother died, two years ago. Before that she did say a few odd words, although

she never spoke much. We didn't see that it was any
cause for worry, though, some children are late in learning to speak.' Rose spoke in a sharp, abrupt manner and
Rachel couldn't help wondering whether this was to
cover her anxiety over Melanie. An anxiety well
founded. Even without her years of experience teaching maladjusted children Rachel would have recognised that there was something very wrong with little
Melanie Duncan.

The next morning was, as Ben had predicted, sunny
and warm. At ten o'clock he called for Rachel as he had
promised. He was wearing jeans and a check shirt which
was open at the neck to reveal a muscular chest smat-
tered with dark hair. He smiled at her, his glance warm
and approving in a friendly way. She had slept well in
the little bedroom under the eaves at her aunt's cottage
and woken refreshed, and she knew she was not unat-
tractive in the simple blue peasant-style dress she had
chosen to wear. Not that she was interested in looking
attractive; there could never be anyone to replace
Keith; nevertheless, she was feminine enough to recog-
nise and appreciate an admiring look.

She locked the door behind her and left the key
under a stone, where Aunt Rose, who had left early to
begin her duties up at the 'Big House' as she called it,
had directed.

'You can see the mountains this morning,' said Ben,
as they walked up the drive towards Kilfinan House.
'Everything's sparkling. Even the colours are brighter.
It's always the same after the rain—as if the world's
been washed and now it's hung out to dry.'

'That's quite poetic,' Rachel smiled, 'although I
must say I agree with you. Things look very different
today, now that the sun's shining. Yesterday, with the
mist hanging so low over them, the mountains just
didn't seem to be there. But today . . .' she gazed around,

'it's incredibly beautiful.' From where she stood Rachel could see the mountains all around her rising, green and tree-covered on the lower slopes, but becoming gradually more wild and craggy as they rose higher and higher. And between the mountains the road snaked through the glen like a length of grey ribbon flung carelessly down.

At the end of the drive stood Kilfinan House, protected by banks of rhododendrons. It was a white, slate-roofed house, with two large urns flanking the steps to the front door. It was not big by some standards—some thirty rooms, Ben told her—but standing as it did on the mountain slope overlooking the glen it was impressive.

'And that's where Alistair Duncan lives,' Rachel breathed. 'It's a big house to live in all alone.'

'Oh, he doesn't live there alone. Richard, his son, lives there too. And Melanie, Richard's daughter.'

'Oh, I didn't realise. . . .'

'You don't know about the family?' Ben cocked an eyebrow at her. 'Come into the barn with me, I want to sharpen some knives, and I'll fill you in briefly before we go on to the house and pick up Melanie. By the way, you don't mind if she comes with us?'

'Of course not.' Rachel followed Ben to the big stone-built barn housing all manner of farm equipment, ranging from the gleaming up-to-date tractor to rusty museum pieces which clearly hadn't seen daylight for decades.

'Now,' Ben rummaged in the drawer of a battered old dresser in the corner and found an oil-stone, put it on the bench and began sharpening his penknife, 'where shall I begin? Old Alistair Duncan—well, he's not that old, barely sixty I should think—owns the whole of Kilfinan Estate, which includes the house and grounds, the two Lodges—Rose lives in one and I live in the other—and several farms up the glen. Richard, his son, also lives at the house but has no part in running the Estate, much to Alistair's alternate sorrow and disgust. Richard preferred to go it alone, rather than step into his father's shoes, and he's built up a business of his own, hiring out fishing boats at Ardenbeg— you'll have come through there on your way here.' He looked up at Rachel and smiled. 'Get the picture so far?'

She nodded. 'And my aunt runs Kilfinan House for them.'

'That's right. Or course she has a bit of help with the heavy work. A woman from the clachan comes in to do that.'

Rachel digested this. 'So Melanie is Richard's daughter,' she said after a moment, adding, 'and Richard's wife is. . . .'

'Dead. Killed in an accident,' Ben spoke roughly. He ceased the circular movement of the knife on the oil-stone and tried the blade with his thumb. 'It was a terrible tragedy. She was beautiful, quite beautiful, Celia Duncan.'

'You admired her,' said Rachel, stating the obvious.

Ben looked past her, through the open door of the barn, to the mountains beyond. 'Aye, you could say that,' he said softly. Then with an obvious effort he turned his attention back to Rachel and said with a smile, 'But what man in his senses doesn't admire a beautiful woman? And I'm lucky enough to be spending the morning in the company of one. Come along, let's collect Melanie and then we'll show you our waterfall. Listen, you can hear it from here.'

As they left the barn Rachel could hear the distant rushing noise.

'I didn't realise that what I could hear was the sound of water, I thought it was the wind in the trees.' She turned to the man beside her. 'Ben, does Melanie miss her mother very much?'

'I should think everyone misses Celia,' he said simply.

They collected Melanie, who led the way up the hill-side, running on ahead, excited in her strange, silent way, and then running back to pull on Ben's hand before running on again.

'All right, poppet, give us time to catch our breath,' he laughed, 'we're coming as quickly as we can!'

They threaded their way among the trees and bracken and Rachel found her feet sinking up to her ankles in enormous cushions of moss, damp from yesterday's rain. Once, Ben stopped to help her climb a gate across their path, holding both her hands to steady her as she jumped down. For a moment before he released her he looked down into her eyes and she saw the warmth in his gaze. She looked away quickly over his shoulder and caught Melanie's expression. The child had watched the perfectly innocent scene, but the look on her face was pure venom. For a moment Rachel was taken aback, then she understood; Melanie was jealous. Ben released her hands and she moved away. Immediately Melanie ran and put her hand in his, looking up at him anxiously.

Thoughtfully, Rachel walked on. It would seem that if she wanted to make a friend of the child she would have to make sure this tall, craggy man didn't pay her too much attention. The thought didn't trouble her; Keith was still too near—not that Ben was the type of man she would have been attracted to anyway.

They carried on up the hillside, the sound of rush-ing water becoming louder and louder, until suddenly Melanie broke away and ran to a flimsy fence.

'Careful, poppet,' Ben called, 'it's a long way down there.'

Rachel followed him to where Melanie stood. The

waterfall was about fifty feet high, and they were standing on the edge of a ravine about halfway up. From high above them the water fell in steps, cascading, it seemed, from boulder to boulder, changing direction as it fell, the force of it capping each boulder with frothy white lace. Below them it fell into a deep stream, green-gladed and cool, the water sparkling spasmodically in the sunlight dappling through the trees above. Rachel caught her breath after a brief moment of dizziness. 'It's beautiful!'

Ben nodded. 'Yes, it is quite something. It's impressive today, too, because of yesterday's rain. Sometimes it's little more than a trickle, and that worries us because this is where all our water comes from.'

Rachel looked at him in amazement.

'Oh, yes,' he smiled, 'we've our own water supply, a complicated system of pipes and filters. It's pretty old, but it works perfectly well. And it all comes from here.' He looked at his watch. 'My, we've been longer than I expected. I've to take Melanie to Ardenbeg to meet her father at twelve and I must have a word with Mr Duncan first. Look, I'll hurry on. Melanie will show you the way down, then perhaps you'd like to come with us to Ardenbeg.'

Melanie pouted.

'I know you don't like going to Dunglevin to see the speech therapist, poppet, but it pleases your daddy to take you. Not that it does a scrap of good,' he added quietly to Rachel. 'Now, I must hurry. Bring Rachel round to the garage, Melanie.'

The child nodded sulkily and Ben hurried off.

Slowly Rachel followed, with Melanie lagging behind. The way was fairly straightforward, which was fortunate because Melanie was no help, deliberately hanging back or going off in the wrong direction.

Rachel made no attempt to stop her; she wandered through the trees full of her own thoughts. She was used to dealing with difficult children, but she realised that if she was going to win this little girl's affection she would have to go about it very carefully. She called, 'I'm going to see if I can reach the garage first, Melanie, even though I don't know the way,' and was gratified by a scuttling in the undergrowth as Melanie began to run.

She found her way to the garage with no trouble. As she approached she could see Ben talking to a distinguished-looking man with grey hair, whom she judged to be Alistair Duncan. Excitedly, Melanie ran up to him and put her arms round his waist. He ruffled her hair absently, at the same time taking something out of his pocket and giving it to her. Then, still deep in conversation with Ben, he began to move away, walking with a marked limp. Melanie, her shoulders drooping, went and got into the estate car standing by, and Rachel climbed in beside her.

'You won,' she said cheerfully. 'But then you know all the short cuts.'

Melanie didn't answer. She sat turning over the pound note her grandfather had given her, her expression bleak.

Rachel felt a surge of compassion towards the little girl.

'What are you going to buy with that?' she asked.

Melanie glared at her, stuffed the note into the pocket of her jeans and turned to gaze out of the window.

Rachel couldn't help comparing the journey to Ardenbeg in bright sunshine with her journey the day before in the company of the taciturn stranger who had nevertheless appeared to know so much about her.

Ben drew her attention to one or two particular points of interest, but in the main he was silent, seeing that she was content simply to drink in the beauty of the surroundings, a beauty that had been obscured the previous day by the mist and rain. Once or twice she sensed Melanie's eyes on her but as soon as she turned to smile and speak the child turned away.

At Ardenbeg, the quaint little town nestling against the foot of the mountain where the loch entered the sea, Rachel could see the road to Dunglevin climbing along the side of the mountain, high above the loch, the cars crawling over it hardly bigger than ants. It wasn't called a scenic road for nothing, Rachel decided; on a day like this the view must extend for miles.

Ben drew into a small car park. 'You can wander round the town if you like, Rachel, while I take Melanie to her father's office,' he suggested.

But, surprisingly, Melanie took Rachel's hand and refused to let go, although she still wouldn't look at her.

'All right, Melanie, Rachel can come too, if that's what you want,' Ben said with a smile.

They made their way to a small office overlooking the loch. There were numerous charts on the walls and the desk was littered with papers. A pair of thigh boots stood in one corner and a thick Arran sweater was flung over the back of a chair. Rachel had taken this much in when a door in the corner opened and Melanie's father came in.

She recognised Richard Duncan immediately; the thick black hair, the long stern face, the dark, deep-set almost navy blue eyes. No wonder he had known so much about her as he drove her to Glencarrick from Dunglevin yesterday. No wonder, either, that he had been lacking in sympathy for her misfortune. Good-

ness knows he had enough sorrow of his own; tragically
losing his beautiful wife and being left to shoulder
alone the burden of his strange little daughter. She
smiled at him as Ben made the introductions, ashamed
that his first impression of her—mistaken though it
was—must have been one of wallowing self-pity.

'We've already met,' he cut Ben short. He let his
gaze rest on her simple summer dress and sandals. 'I
notice that you've taken full advantage of the fact that
the sun is shining today, despite your alleged indifference to the weather the last time we met,' he remarked.

Rachel flushed. She had been prepared to forgive
his outspoken comments yesterday, prepared even to
feel sorry for him in his misfortune, but the man was
downright rude. And arrogant!

Without giving her time to reply he turned his
attention to Melanie. 'Are you ready, child?' he asked,
not unkindly.

Melanie shook her head vehemently, still clutching
Rachel's hand, and Rachel could feel the sudden tension in the little figure. She knelt down so that her
face was on a level with Melanie's and saw that the
child's eyes were full of terror.

'There's no need to be frightened of going to see the
speech therapist, darling,' she said softly. 'She only
wants to help you. Surely you want to be able to talk,
don't you?'

'She's being utterly ridiculous, as usual,' Richard
said impatiently. He fished a tie out of a drawer in his
desk and knotted it expertly without the aid of a
mirror. 'Come along, child, I haven't all day to waste.'

The four of them left the office, Richard leading the
way, with Ben following him and Melanie, still clutching Rachel's hand, bringing up the rear. Rachel talked
encouragingly to the little girl all the way to the car,

which she climbed into without further protest, but
Rachel was dismayed to see tears well up in the big
brown eyes as she fastened the safety belt for her.

'Why is she so frightened of the speech therapist?'
Rachel managed to say to Richard before he got into
the driver's seat.

'I can't imagine. Miss Botham is a motherly soul and
does her best. She doesn't seem to be having any success, though.' He looked down at his little daughter, a
look of exasperation on his face. 'Sometimes I think
it's sheer stubbornness that prevents her from speaking.' Suddenly he turned away, his shoulders drooping.
He took off the glasses he wore for driving and passed
his hands over his eyes; the gesture was one of weariness and defeat and Rachel caught a look of hope-
lessness in his eyes before he climbed in beside his
daughter, his glasses and his aloof, businesslike veneer
both safely back in place.

But in that brief moment Rachel had glimpsed
the real Richard Duncan; had seen the loneliness and
heartache kept carefully hidden behind the hard shell
he presented to the world and had realised how he
must have loved Celia, his wife, and how he must miss
her. Just as she missed Keith, her dead fiancé.

But the face before her eyes as Ben drove her back to
Glencarrick was not that of Keith but of Richard, who,
in those few unguarded seconds, had revealed more of
himself than he suspected. More, too, than Rachel had
wished to see, for without that brief glimpse she could
have disliked him wholeheartedly, whereas now....

Mentally, she gave herself a shake. She had come
to Glencarrick to mend a broken heart, not to have it
broken all over again.

CHAPTER TWO

THE days slipped quickly by and Rachel had been staying at Kilfinan Lodge a week almost before she knew it. She spent quite a lot of time on her own because her aunt was usually occupied up at the Big House, but she was happy enough exploring the countryside. Wandering round the Estate she often saw Ben at work and she would stop and have a friendly chat with him, careful not to antagonise Melanie, who was never far away.

Since the day at Ardenbeg when she had clung so tenaciously to her Melanie had taken little interest in Rachel, but she kept a watchful eye on Ben and if she considered he was paying too much attention to Rachel she would slip between them and slide her hand proprietorially into his. Rachel was puzzled. She was used to dealing with difficult children but she had never met anyone quite like Melanie.

'Has she always been like this, Ben?' she asked one day. She had come upon Ben fixing a fence by the stream and had been watching him in silence for some time before she spoke. He was stripped to the waist, working as he was in a sheltered pocket of sunshine, and his back was broad and tanned. He straightened up and glanced at the little girl, who was gathering daisies a little distance away.

'She hasn't spoken a word since around the time her mother died. Mind you, she was never what you'd call a chatterbox—not like some children.'

'But she *could* talk.'

'Oh, yes, she *could* talk, but she was always a quiet

little thing.' He regarded her thoughtfully. 'I suppose she used to talk to me more than anyone.'

'Have you tried to *make* her talk?' Rachel asked.

Ben shook his head. 'I don't think that's the way to go about it. She'll talk when she's ready and not before. I expect it was the shock of her mother's death that caused it and it'll right itself in time. Richard takes her for speech therapy—he knows it's a waste of time and money but he does it just the same, to salve his conscience, I suppose. Then there's the row going on over sending her to school; Richard wants to send her to boarding school, but the old man favours a governess,' he grinned, 'that's an old-fashioned word, isn't it? Alistair thinks she's been upset enough, without sending her away from everyone she knows, but Richard thinks that would be best for her.' He rubbed the back of his hand across his forehead. 'Something will have to be done about her soon, that's for sure. They can't shelve the problem for much longer.'

Rachel frowned. 'But surely it's up to Richard. After all, Melanie's his daughter.'

'It's not as simple as that,' Ben told her. 'Richard's business is not making enough money to pay the fees of the school he has in mind. So without Alistair's financial blessing she can't be sent there. Maybe the old man is using this as a lever to get Richard back running the Estate, because that's what he would like more than anything.'

'Poor little girl,' Rachel murmured. 'It's sad to think she's being used as a pawn.' She wandered over to where Melanie was sitting, her lap full of daisies, and sat down beside her.

'I used to make daisy chains when I was a little girl,' she said, picking a few daisies and stringing them together as she spoke. 'It's quite easy. You can make necklaces, bracelets, even a little coronet. See?' She made a circlet of the flowers and laid it gently on Melanie's dark hair.

The child put up her hand and felt the flowers on her head. For a moment she almost smiled; then she snatched them off and scrambled to her feet, daisies spilling in all directions, and ran off.

Rachel stood up and went thoughtfully on her way. There must be some way of getting through to the unhappy little girl.

It was little more than two miles to Ardenbeg by the mountain track, although three times this distance by road, and so deep in thought was she that Rachel had crossed the mountain and was down by the little harbour at Ardenbeg before she realised where her feet had taken her. She stood watching the boats; the pleasure steamer, plying between the lochs and the little islands at the mouth of the Clyde; the small sailing boats bobbing on the wind-rippled water and a larger fishing vessel—the *Celia*—just coming in to moor. It was a warm day, but here by the water there was enough breeze to make Rachel wish she had brought a sweater to put on over her smock-top and jeans.

She watched absently as several men disembarked from the fishing boat, most of them carrying fishing rods in one hand and a 'bend' of mackerel in the other. The last man to disembark, some time after the others, was Richard Duncan.

He clomped along the jetty in thigh-boots and thick Arran sweater, yellow oilskins over his arm, and Rachel couldn't help noticing the young, almost boyish look about him today. He stopped when he saw her and ran his fingers through his tousled hair.

'Rachel! What are you doing here? Did Ben bring you?'

She couldn't help smiling at his surprise. 'Of course not. I walked. It's not far by the mountain track.'

'That was a stupid thing to do.'

'Why? I enjoyed it. I love walking.'

He stopped and turned to look at her. 'One of the first things you must learn is that you don't go marching willy-nilly over these hills. You obviously haven't realised just how quickly the mists can come down. Come back to my office with me and wait until I've changed, then I'll take you home in my car.'

She opened her mouth to protest, but he walked on, giving her little choice but to follow him, seething inside to think that she had made herself look foolish.

They walked along in silence and Rachel realised that although she herself was considered quite tall she barely reached Richard Duncan's shoulder. Suddenly he looked down at her again. 'There's a Mini in the garage at Kilfinan House. True, it hasn't been used much lately, but I'll ask Ben to check it over and then you can have the use of it. You do drive, I take it?'

She nodded. 'Oh, yes.'

'Right. It'll make you mobile so you don't have to go clambering over mountain tracks. *That's* for people who know what they're doing.'

'I'm not a complete idiot!' Rachel was stung to retort.

'Then in future don't act like one. Look.' He pointed to the way she had come from Glencarrick. Not only was the track obscured, but the mountain, shrouded in a thick mist, had completely disappeared. It was as if it had never existed. 'It'll clear as quickly as it came, but if you were up there now you wouldn't be feeling too happy,' he said.

She shuddered. Of course, he was right.

When they arrived at Richard's office there was already someone there waiting for him. The visitor was a girl of around Rachel's own age, with chestnut hair, thickly coiled into the nape of her neck, and a flawless, peaches-and-cream complexion. She got to her feet as they entered and the thing that struck Rachel was not her beauty—although there was no denying that—but her air of complete self-possession. She was wearing a pale green jump suit that moulded her figure to its best advantage, with a darker green scarf knotted with studied carelessness at the neck. The effect was striking.

'You're late back, Richard,' she greeted him. 'I've been here waiting nearly half an hour.'

'I'm sorry, but you know I'm unpredictable, Moira. The lines got fouled up on a wreck, that's what made us late. It was my fault, I should have checked the chart myself instead of leaving it to someone else.' He sat down and begun pulling off his boots. 'Did you want to see me for anything special?'

Moira didn't speak for a moment. She simply gazed expectantly at Rachel.

'Oh,' Richard took the hint and made the introductions. 'Rachel Canfield—staying with her aunt, Rose Canfield, at the Lodge; Moira McLeod, farms at the top of the glen with her brother.'

Moira nodded to Rachel with a wry smile. 'With my brother *when* he's at home, I might add. Most of his time is spent in London where he's hoping to make a small fortune as a playwright.' She made a face. 'So far, the fortune he's made has been *very* small, in fact practically non-existent.'

'That's a bit uncharitable, Moira,' said Richard. 'David did have one success, remember.'

'Yes, and it was on the strength of that that he uprooted himself and went to London. Maybe it would have been better if he'd never sold that first play—he hasn't sold one since.'

'Have you heard from him lately?' Richard asked.

'Yes, I had a letter this morning. He says he's coming home for the Midsummer Ball at the end of next week and will I find him a partner. That's why I called on you today, Richard, to make sure you hadn't forgotten that you're taking me.'

'I hadn't forgotten.' Richard peeled off two layers of sweater to reveal a navy sports shirt and ran a comb through his hair. 'But who have you got lined up for David?'

'Nobody, so far. By the time I'd exhausted his list of who *not* to ask I find there's nobody much left.' She turned to Rachel. 'Perhaps you'd like to come?'

Receiving such an offhand invitation Rachel's first instinct was to refuse, but then she caught the look on Richard's face. Clearly, this was just what he was expecting her to do so, perversely, she smiled at Moira and said quietly, 'Thank you, I'll be happy to come. It's nice of you to ask me.'

'Good. It's a relief to get that settled. Mind you, you'll find David good company. He can be quite a charmer —when he chooses.' Moira turned her attention to Richard and linked her arm possessively through his. 'I've half an hour to spare, Rick. Have you time for some tea at Craig Lodge before we go our separate ways?'

'I'm sorry, Moira.' Richard extricated himself from her clasp and began sorting through the papers on his desk. 'I have work to do back at the house; besides, I've arranged to give Rachel a lift back to Glencarrick. Some other time, maybe.'

Moira sighed deeply. 'You work far too hard, my dear.' She picked up her bag and went to the door.

'But don't forget you're dining with me next Thursday, work or no work.'

'I shan't forget,' he replied, without looking up.

When Moira had gone, leaving behind her a faint but distinctive waft of expensive perfume, totally out of place among the sea-boots and fishing tackle of Richard's office, Rachel sat down and prepared to wait for Richard.

'Moira is very beautiful,' she remarked after a few moments.

'Mm? Yes, I suppose she is quite attractive.' He spoke absently.

Rachel stared at him. It was clear that he was completely oblivious of the fact that Moira McLeod was in love with him. What a wonderful person Celia, his wife, must have been if even now, two years after her death, he still had eyes for no other woman. But watching his dark head bent over the desk Rachel could well believe it might be so. He looked the kind of man who would not love lightly, but his love, once given, would be complete and would demand nothing less in return.

An involuntary sigh escaped her and he looked up.

'You've been very patient,' he said. 'I've finished now, so we'll be on our way.' As he spoke he smiled, a smile that transformed his habitually stern features. Suddenly it was not difficult to see why Moira McLeod was in love with him.

Rachel followed him to the car and they drove off.

'Ben tells me you've worked with ...' he hesitated, '... difficult children.' His eyes were firmly on the road ahead as he spoke.

'That's right. Until ... recently I was teaching in a school for maladjusted children.'

'Melanie's not maladjusted,' he said quickly. 'She was perfectly all right until two years ago; a quiet child, but normal enough. She's only been like this since—since her mother died.'

He spoke those last words roughly and Rachel noticed that his knuckles showed white on the steering wheel.

'It was a shattering experience for her. And for you,' she couldn't help adding.

His reply, if he made one, was drowned in the sound of his horn as he honked at a silly sheep that trotted across the path of the car and he didn't speak again until he stopped the car outside Kilfinan Cottage.

'I wonder. . . .' He turned the engine off and shifted in his seat to look at her, his dark eyes troubled, 'Maybe if *you* talked to Melanie. Maybe, in time. . . .' He passed his hand across his forehead. 'Miss Botham, the speech therapist, doesn't seem to be having any success at all.'

Rachel frowned. 'I've so little time here. I'm only here for a holiday, you know. I have to go home in a few weeks.'

He nodded briskly. 'Yes, of course. I was forgetting.' He leaned across and opened her door for her and as he did so she could smell the tang of the sea clinging to him. 'School, of course, is the answer. She should be sent away to school.'

'If you did that she might feel that you were rejecting her altogether,' Rachel said thoughtfully. She smiled. 'She's obviously very attached to Ben, I've seen her with him several times. . . .'

Richard started up the car. 'As you say, you're only here for a holiday. Melanie's not your problem, so there's no need for you to worry about her.' His mood seemed to have changed abruptly and he was impatient to be off.

Rachel got out of the car. 'That's not what I meant at all and you know it,' she said. 'If I can help with

Melanie I will, but it would be a mistake to gain her confidence and then go away and leave her.'

'Yes, of course, you're right.' Richard drove off, leaving Rachel to gaze after him. She felt so sorry for him; even with so many people around he was a solitary figure, and she wished there was some way she could help, but however hard she tried, whenever she was with him she always seemed to end up saying or doing the wrong thing. Was she simply tactless, or was it just that he heartily disliked her?

'You're very quiet tonight, my girl.' Aunt Rose was sitting on one side of the fire in the cosy cottage kitchen, crocheting busily, while Rachel sat on the other, a book in her hand, gazing into the fire, which, although the day had been warm, was cheerful and bright. Rachel looked up; her thoughts had been far away on her conversation with Richard earlier. 'Mind,' Rose went on, 'I believe your holiday is doing you good. You're certainly beginning to look healthier—in fact, I believe you're putting on weight.'

'Oh, Auntie, I hope not,' Rachel laughed. 'That would mean I'd have to cut down on your delicious baking, and I'd hate that.'

Aunt Rose smiled. 'It's good to hear you laugh. There was barely a smile on your face when you first came. You like it here?'

'I love it. But who wouldn't? It's all so incredibly beautiful.'

'*She* didn't.'

Rachel looked up, startled at the vehemence in her aunt's tone.

'Who do you mean?'

'Why, Richard's wife, of course. She hated it.' Aunt Rose's crochet hook seemed to fly even faster as she spoke. 'Said she found it boring. Missed the social life she'd been used to. She should never have ... but never mind.' She looked up at Rachel and smiled. 'Tell me about the family, my girl. It's so long since I saw your father.'

Although she was puzzled at the older woman's outburst Rachel took the hint and didn't question her further. 'You could come back with me to see them; I know Dad would love to see you,' she suggested. 'And I'm sure you could do with a holiday. Sometimes you don't look at all well. Are you working too hard, Auntie? Or worrying too much over Melanie?'

Aunt Rose nodded. 'It's true, I do worry over the child, she's been through so much.'

'She misses her mother?'

'She spends far too much time running wild over the Estate. She's becoming like a wild creature, like the roe-deer that you glimpse in the woods.'

'Ben seems to understand her. She loves to be with him, it seems.'

'Ben is the last person she should trust.'

'Whatever do you mean, Auntie?' Rachel asked in surprise.

'Nothing. Nothing at all.' Rose gathered up her crocheting and busied herself with the supper.

Rachel didn't question her further. It was obvious from her manner that her aunt had already said more than she had intended. But she was puzzled.

The next day Rachel went up to the Big House, as Rose called it, with her aunt, and Rose proudly showed her over it. All the rooms were cared for in strict rotation, even the parts that were seldom used. One wing was like a small stately home, furnished with priceless antiques and pictures. The wing that the family lived in, however, had deep comfortable armchairs, colour television and stereo equipment. To Rachel it was like stepping from one world into another. Kilfinan House and its occupants was clearly all Rose lived for, and she told Rachel how she had been nanny to Richard as a small boy, living-in at the house. It was not until Richard had married that she had been given her own cottage at the end of the drive.

'Alistair would like me to come back here, now that Celia's dead,' she said, 'but I must say I like having my own front door; I should have done it years ago, but we just didn't think. Anyway, it makes no difference to the way I run the house.'

'Whose idea was it that you should move to the cottage, then?' Rachel asked.

'Celia's, of course.'

Rachel was rapidly gaining the impression that however highly esteemed Celia had been by everyone else, Aunt Rose had definitely not fallen under her spell.

Pondering this, she left her aunt immersed in account books and slipped away to the garage to have a look at the Mini that Richard had suggested putting at her disposal—if he had remembered his offer.

Obviously he had. Ben was there, his head under the bonnet, tinkering with the engine. He straightened up when she greeted him and wiped his hands on an oily rag.

'She seems to be in good order,' he said, his teeth showing even and white in his tanned face as he smiled at her. 'I was just going to take her for a test run and then she's all yours.' He slammed down the bonnet and got in behind the wheel. 'Coming?'

She didn't need asking twice.

'Nobody's driven this car much,' said Ben, running through the gears. 'It was bought to replace Celia's car, which was a complete write-off.' He jammed on the brakes viciously. 'I don't know why they bothered. Celia's no longer here to drive it; Richard's got his own car and when Alistair wants a car he usually takes the truck.'

'What exactly happened to Celia?' Rachel couldn't resist the question. 'I know she had an accident, but. . . .'

'Her car ran off the road—why, heaven knows. She was a good driver and she knew the road to Dunglevin like the back of her hand. True, it was fairly late at night, but all the same, it should never have happened.' He spoke savagely and Rachel could see the speedometer creeping up and up. It was quite plain that Ben had held Celia Duncan in high esteem.

'What was she like? Celia, I mean?'

He relaxed and the needle began to drop to a reasonable speed. 'I think she was the most beautiful woman I ever saw,' he said softly.

'Is Melanie like her mother?'

'A little. Of course, she's dark, like her father. Celia was fair; flaxen, almost.' He fell silent and didn't speak again until they were driving down the narrow main street at Ardenbeg. Then he said, 'Have you seen the magnificent view from the Dunglevin road?'

She shook her head. 'The last time I was on that road was in a blinding rainstorm.'

'I'll take you up and show you, then. It's worth seeing.' He drove through Ardenbeg and began climbing the narrow road cut along the side of the mountain. There was just room for two cars to pass, but it was a perilously close thing. And below, far below, the loch sparkled in the morning sunlight. For about two miles the road climbed, sometimes steeply, sometimes more gently, until, high above the loch and the little town of Ardenbeg, the road widened out on to a natural plateau big enough for about half a dozen cars to park.

Ben parked the Mini and they both got out and went to lean on the railings that fenced in three sides of the area. Away into the distance towards the mouth of the Clyde stretched the loch, dotted with islands, some green and wooded, some quite barren. Here and there tiny boats bobbed on the waves.

'Look down there,' said Ben, pointing to a spot directly below where they were standing. There, almost hidden by the trees and bushes that grew on the lower slopes of the mountain, was another, larger island and there were several boats moored in its shelter. Beside the island, on a finger of land jutting out from the mainland, stood a tiny lighthouse.

'The lighthouse is derelict now,' Ben said, 'but it's a favourite spot for picnickers.'

'How on earth do you reach it?' As far as Rachel could see the spot was quite isolated.

'Three ways. By the low coast road from Ardenbeg; by boat; or, if you're really intrepid, by that path.' He pointed to a narrow track disappearing into the undergrowth down the mountainside on the other side of the fence. 'Look, there's a stile to reach it by.'

'It's an awful long way down,' Rachel said with a shudder.

'It is that.' Ben laid his arm carelessly across her shoulders. 'I'll take you down there one day. But not today.' He glanced at his watch, 'We must be getting back. I'm not on holiday even if you are. There's work waiting for me to do.' He held open the driver's door. 'Come on, now, you drive and I'll admire the view. You'll find she handles fairly easily.'

Rachel drove back to Glencarrick without any difficulty, but she was conscious all the time of Ben's arm, laid lightly across the back of her seat, his hand brushing her shoulder. This disturbed her, although she didn't know why. She didn't understand Ben, but she was becoming increasingly convinced that what he had felt for Richard's wife had been more than simply admiration. Could he have been in love with her? The more Rachel learned about the dead Celia the more of an enigma she became.

CHAPTER THREE

RACHEL found the Mini useful for exploring the countryside around Ardenbeg and Glencarrick. It was all very beautiful and she could feel its relaxing and therapeutic effect on her. No longer did she feel that familiar clutch of cold panic when she thought of the years stretching ahead of her without Keith. She was beginning to feel that life was still worth living in spite of everything that had happened to her. Yet she didn't feel ready to return home and pick up the threads of her former life. She had become intrigued by the people she had met at Kilfinan House—by poor mixed-up little Melanie, who there was not time to help because it would be cruel to gain her confidence and then leave her; by Ben; what could Aunt Rose have against him? He was so good-natured and likeable—how convenient it would be to fall in love with him and live happily ever after. Rachel smiled. This was simply not possible, Ben was not her type, pleasant company though he was. Anyway, Rachel was becoming increasingly certain that Celia had been the love of his life. Celia. There was an enigma. And the more Rachel discovered about Richard's wife the more confused she became. Aunt Rose had indicated that she had been unhappy at Kilfinan House, with some disapproval, Rachel couldn't help feeling. Yet Celia had stayed there. Perhaps no sacrifice had been too great for Celia to make for her husband. As for Richard, it was plain he had never recovered from his wife's untimely death. But when he did Moira McLeod would be there, waiting.

All this was going through her mind as she dressed for the Midsummer Ball. She had found out from Richard that it was to be held at the Caladh Hotel at Ardenbeg and she was thankful she had brought a suitable dress with her, although she hadn't expected to need it in such a remote part of Scotland.

The dress was of a soft, silky material in deep coral. Sleeveless, the skirt fell away from the closely-fitting bodice in soft folds, and the high mandarin collar was edged with silver to match her evening bag. It was a simple design, but with her blonde hair loose and shining and a hint of a sparkle of anticipation in her eyes Rachel couldn't help but be pleased with the reflection in her mirror. She went downstairs to wait for Richard, who was going to pick her up before calling at the McLeods' farm for Moira and her brother David, Rachel's partner for the evening.

'You're looking bonny, my girl,' said Aunt Rose when she saw her. She got up out of her chair and came over to her niece and kissed her. 'Enjoy yourself, now. You cannot live in the past, remember,' she said softly. Then as if embarrassed by her show of emotion she gave Rachel's gossamer evening shawl an impatient twitch and said sharply, 'You'll catch your death with only that flimsy thing. The nights can be cold in these parts, you know.'

'Don't worry, I'll be warm enough, Auntie,' Rachel laughed. 'Oh, there's Richard's car. Goodbye. Don't wait up for me.'

'That I shan't,' Aunt Rose retorted. 'There's no telling what time you'll arrive home.'

Richard looked incredibly handsome in evening dress and Rachel couldn't help wishing that she was to have been partnered by him instead of David McLeod, about whom she knew nothing at all.

They stopped for drinks at the McLeod farm and there Rachel met Moira's brother for the first time. He was tall, almost as tall as Richard, and his carefully groomed hair, almost the same chestnut shade as Moira's, hung thick and straight almost to his collar, with a fringe that he flicked back with an impatient gesture of his hand at frequent intervals. He wore square, gold-framed spectacles which gave him a studious, little-boy-lost look, although Rachel estimated that he must be aged around thirty.

There was open admiration in his eyes as they were introduced and he kept the hand Rachel offered him a shade longer than was necessary. She smiled at him and prepared for an evening of harmless flirtation.

Moira looked stunning. Her dress was of midnight blue, with a low halter neckline. She was wearing her hair piled on top of her head in a complicated style that must have taken her hairdresser hours to do. Round her neck she wore three ropes of pearls. With a pang of something approaching envy Rachel thought what a handsome couple she and Richard made as they chatted together over the drinks that David had poured.

When it was time to go Moira picked up her fur wrap and handed it to Richard to place round her shoulders. 'Are you bringing your car, David?' she asked, taking a last, satisfied glance in the hall mirror on the way to the door.

'There's no need. There'll be plenty of room for us all in mine,' Richard said quickly. Rachel was glad, she wasn't sure why.

The Midsummer Ball was the biggest event in Ardenbeg, apart from the Hogmanay celebrations. The ballroom at the hotel was gaily decorated with balloons and there were flowers everywhere. Even the musicians on the dais at the end of the hall were colourful in full Highland dress. It was all very festive. The big french windows all along one wall of the ballroom had been flung open and there were chairs and tables on the terrace for those who preferred to sit and enjoy the view of the loch and the distant mountains by moonlight.

David danced well, although Rachel wished he wouldn't hold her quite so closely. As the evening wore on, even with the french windows open the atmosphere in the ballroom made her head ache.

'Come out on to the terrace and I'll get you a drink,' he said, taking her arm and guiding her to a small table tucked in a corner behind a large, strategically placed cheese plant.

She sat down gratefully and looked out over the bay, watching the reflected lights from the shore and from the boats at anchor dancing in the restless water of the loch. Her home in Suffolk and the tragic events associated with it seemed light years away. She almost wished she would never have to return.

'I can't see Richard and Moira anywhere.' David put two tall glasses on the table and sat down beside her. 'Not that I looked very hard,' he added, grinning. 'I'd far rather have you all to myself. Cheers!' He lifted his glass. 'Now, tell me all about yourself.'

She shrugged. 'It won't make very interesting listening.' Nevertheless, she found herself telling the man beside her all about Keith and the tragic way her hopes and dreams had been shattered with his death in the plane crash.

He listened, his eyes fixed on a point far out on the loch. 'How long is it since the plane crashed?' he asked when she'd finished.

'Nearly seven months.'

He turned and looked at her, taking her hand in his as he did so. 'That episode in your life is over; finished. Keith is gone and nothing will alter that. You can't waste your life living with what might have been.' He shook his head. 'Nobody is worth that,' he said vehemently, 'But nobody. Life is meant to be enjoyed.' He pulled her to her feet. 'I enjoy life. I'm doing what I want to do. My plays may not exactly set the town alight at the moment, but they will one day, you'll see. Life in London is exciting. That's where it's all happening.'

'But what about your farm? How do you manage to combine writing plays in London with running a farm five hundred miles away?'

'My sister runs the farm. She runs it efficiently and well. She has the right people working for her and things are going exactly the way she wants them to.' He brushed his hand across his forehead in a characteristic gesture. 'Moira has always wanted the farm to herself and she's got it—well, more or less, anyway. At least, she can run it as she chooses, I only put in the occasional appearance and I never interfere.' He drained his glass. 'You don't know my sister very well yet, Rachel, but when you do you'll realise that she knows what she wants and she usually gets it. A very determined woman, my sister.'

Rachel was silent for a while. David's last statement seemed to have a warning ring, for some reason. She gazed thoughtfully at the loch and the mountains beyond, bathed in soft moonlight. 'I still can't believe that you prefer the smoke and grime of London to all this——' she shook her head in disbelief. 'It's so incredibly peaceful and beautiful.'

'Yes, it is beautiful,' he said softly. She looked up at

his tone and found his eyes were not on the loch at all but on her. 'Let's dance.' He took her in his arms and held her close to him. 'Why waste time talking?'

He guided her across the terrace, between the other couples who were dancing in the open air and back into the ballroom. He really was charming, Rachel reflected; Moira had been quite right about her brother. And he was making no secret of the fact that he found her attractive; even now she could feel his cheek against her hair. Yet, for some reason, his attentions left her quite unmoved. What was wrong with her? Had Keith's death robbed her of the ability to feel anything but pain ever again?

At the end of the dance Richard came over to them.

'I think you can relinquish Rachel to me for one dance, David,' he remarked. 'You've monopolised her for the whole of the evening so far.'

'Just one, then. After all, she is my partner for the evening,' said David. 'I'll go and buy my sister a duty drink. Where is she, by the way?'

'Gone to repair her make-up, I believe, although it looked all right to me.' Richard took Rachel's hand and drew her to him. He danced well, their steps matching perfectly, but Rachel was barely conscious that they were dancing at all. The effect on her as he took her in his arms had been immediate and shattering, making her senses reel and her pulses race. Never, ever, had anyone had this effect on her before. She stole a glance at him once, certain that he must be aware of the feelings he had aroused in her, but he was staring ahead, concentrating on guiding her round the crowded floor, occasionally catching her closely to him to avoid colliding with another couple. She, for her part, was only conscious of his body, lean and hard against hers, his arm circling her waist and his hand in hers. Nothing else was real, nothing else mattered. When the dance was over he seemed to hold her to him for a brief second—or was it just her imagination?—before he looked down at her and asked, 'You've time for a drink with me before I hand you back to David? He seems very determined not to let you out of his sight for long.'

'Thank you, a long, cool drink would be nice.' She hoped he would put her breathlessness down to the exertion of dancing and not guess its real cause.

He put his hand lightly under her elbow and guided her across to the bar, and although his fingers were cool his touch seemed to burn into her flesh.

She sipped the drink he brought to her gratefully and by the time David and Moira joined them a moment or two later had managed to regain a little of her composure.

The rest of the evening passed in a daze for Rachel. David was attentive and she managed to flirt mildly with him; yet always she was conscious of Richard. He didn't ask her to dance again and she couldn't help noticing the possessive way Moira clung to him. 'A very determined woman, my sister, she knows what she wants and she usually gets it!' David's words kept hammering through her brain. Yet she could see nothing in Richard's attitude to Moira that was anything other than polite and friendly; it was quite plain that he was still too much in love with his dead wife to think of remarriage. But when he did Moira would be there, waiting.

Suddenly Rachel hated Moira McLeod.

After the Ball the four of them went back to the McLeod farm for coffee and then Richard drove Rachel back to her aunt's house.

'I hope you had a pleasant evening,' he said as he pulled up outside the cottage. 'You seemed rather preoccupied at times, I thought.'

Rachel caught her breath. Richard was too observant by far. She managed a light laugh. 'I had a lovely evening, thank you. How could I help enjoying myself, in such pleasant company?'

'Good. I must say you appeared to get on very well with David McLeod.'

'He's ... charming.'

'He can be, when he likes.' Richard got out of the car abruptly and came round to her side to open the door for her. She stepped out and as she did so she caught her foot in the hem of her dress and would have fallen if he hadn't caught her in his arms. She leaned against him, struggling to regain both her balance and her composure.

'I'm sorry,' she said breathlessly, 'I caught my foot. ...'

For a brief moment she was held against him in a vice-like grip, then, suddenly, he released her. 'You've forgotten your wrap,' he said coolly, reaching beyond her into the car for her evening shawl.

'Thank you.' She took it from him and hurried into the cottage without a backward glance. One thing was certain, Richard Duncan must never know the shattering effect he had on her. That would be just too humiliating.

The lights were still ablaze as she let herself into the cottage. It was nice of Aunt Rose to wait up, but Rachel would have preferred to go straight to her room. She went slowly to the living room, trying to collect her thoughts as she went. Aunt Rose would be eager to hear about the evening, but all Rachel could remember was dancing with Richard and the feel of his arms around her. She pushed open the door.

'Hullo, Auntie....' her voice trailed off. 'Auntie, what's happened?'

Rose was lying on the floor, a chair with one leg smashed off beside her, her face grey with pain. Rachel went and knelt beside her.

'I think it's my back,' Rose's voice was barely above a whisper, '... curtain stuck ... got up to free it ... chair broke ... lying here hours....' She tried a twisted smile. 'Sorry, my girl ... spoiled your evening.' She closed her eyes, exhausted from the effort of speaking.

Rachel damped a sponge and gently wiped her aunt's face. 'I mustn't try to move you to try and make you more comfortable, dear, I could do even more damage. I'm going to ring for help. I won't be a minute.'

She got to her feet and went to the telephone in the hall to ring Kilfinan House.

Richard answered. He listened to what she had to say and then replied, 'I'll ring Archie Murdoch—he's a personal friend of my father as well as a very good doctor. Then I'll join you at the cottage.'

Rachel put down the receiver and went back to her aunt. She was almost unconscious from the pain in her back and Rachel felt completely helpless; there was absolutely nothing she could do to help Rose. She knelt beside her and took her hand. The older woman's eyes flickered open and a ghost of a smile crossed her face. 'Glad you're here, my girl,' she whispered. Then her eyes closed again.

Richard arrived, full of gentle concern for his old nanny. This was yet another side to his character, Rachel discovered. Then Archie Murdoch came, a small, grey-bearded, twinkling-eyed man who seemed somehow to ease the situation by just being there. He examined Rose with infinite care.

Then, 'It's hospital for you, my lass,' he said cheerfully. 'All your limbs seem reasonably mobile, that's
one good thing, but until we can take some X-rays it's
impossible to tell what the damage is.'

A look of alarm crossed Rose's face.

'Don't worry, lass,' he smiled his puckish smile and
was rewarded by an answering glimmer from Rose,
'we'll put ye right, but until we can take the pictures
there's no telling how long it will take. Now carefully,'
he spoke to the ambulance men who had just arrived.
'Don't jar or twist her. That's it, easy, easy now.' He
turned to Rachel, who had taken the opportunity to
slip upstairs and change into jeans and sweater while
her aunt was being moved. 'You'll be going with her,
young lady?'

'Yes, of course.'

'Good. I'll follow in my car.'

The ambulance journey seemed an interminable
nightmare; every bump in the road causing Rose to
wince or groan in spite of the pain-killing injection
Archie Murdoch had given her, and there was nothing
Rachel could do but hold her aunt's hand and watch
helplessly. But at last it was over and they reached
the cottage hospital at Dunglevin. Soon Rachel saw
Rose comfortably established in a small ward with one
other bed in it so she would have someone to talk to
when she felt well enough.

By the time Rachel was ready to leave it was five a.m.
She stood on the steps of the hospital, amazed that it
was daylight, and realised, for the first time, that she
had no means of getting back to Glencarrick.

Then a voice at her elbow asked, 'Rose is comfortable? You're ready to go home?' and Richard, still in
evening dress, was beside her.

'Richard!' She passed her hand over her eyes in

disbelief. 'How long have you been here?'

'I brought up the rear in the convoy. I followed Archie's car following the ambulance.' He smiled down at her sympathetically. 'It was rather a rough ride for Rose, wasn't it?'

She nodded.

He squeezed her arm gently. 'She's in good hands now. Archie Murdoch's the best there is. There's nothing more you can do. Come along. My car's over there, I'll take you home, you look about all in.'

He spoke gently, almost tenderly, and as he led her to the car the tensions of the past few hours, coupled with weariness, overtook her and she burst into tears.

'It's all right. Rose will be all right,' he whispered, gathering her to him and holding her close. 'But it's all been a bit much for you, hasn't it?'

He talked on, quietly, until her tears subsided. She didn't know what he was saying, all she was aware of was the smooth feel of his dinner jacket, the faint tang still clinging of his after-shave and the touch of his hand on her hair as his arms cradled her. Finally, he tilted up her face.

'Better now?' As he looked down at her suddenly the gentle compassion left his eyes, to be replaced by a fierce hungry longing such as Rachel had never seen before. For one wild moment she thought he was going to kiss her and she held her breath, her senses reeling. But he released her and turned away, saying abruptly, 'Right, then, we'll be on our way.'

He drove back to Glencarrick at break-neck speed, hardly speaking a word, his jaw set like granite. It was as if he was ashamed of his flash of tenderness towards her, annoyed that he had allowed her to penetrate his armour of hardness.

As for Rachel, she had glimpsed the man behind the

armour, and seen the hunger in his eyes. If she had fancied herself in love with Richard Duncan before she was now utterly and completely under his spell. She knew it could bring her nothing but heartache.

He pulled up outside the cottage.

'Go to bed now,' he commanded, 'and sleep for as long as you can. I'll see you're not disturbed.'

'What about Melanie and—everything?' Rachel was so exhausted she hardly knew what she was saying.

'She's not your problem. Just go to bed and sleep.'

'All right. Thank you.' She got out of the car, noticing that Richard looked as exhausted as she felt, but she made no comment. He was not her problem, either, as he would be only too quick to tell her.

She let herself into the cottage and went upstairs to bed.

She slept until three in the afternoon, then she got up and had a leisurely bath, after first phoning the cottage hospital.

'Your aunt is as comfortable as can be expected,' a Scottish voice told her. 'But I'm afraid it's a broken pelvis she has. She'll need to stay here and have complete bed-rest for some time.'

Some time. What did that mean? Rachel asked herself as she relaxed in a warm perfumed bath. Days? Weeks? Months? And what about her, Rachel? Should she stay on at Kilfinan Cottage or would she simply be in the way? She had been in Scotland less than a month, but was it time she went back home and picked up the threads of her former life?

She climbed out of the bath and towelled herself dry; common sense dictated that that was the best course. A vision of Richard Duncan rose before her. Best to get out before it was too late. To stay on at Glencarrick was only to invite heartbreak.

She went downstairs and scrambled herself some eggs, and she was just washing up after this when there was a knock at the door.

It was Richard. He looked tired and faintly irritable. 'May I come in and talk to you?' he asked, running his fingers through his hair in what, in anyone else, would have seemed a nervous gesture. 'I know I said I'd see you weren't disturbed, but ... have you had a good sleep?'

'Oh, yes,' she laughed ruefully, 'I didn't wake till three this afternoon. How about you?'

'I had a couple of hours.' He yawned. 'It's catching up on me now, though.'

'Would you like some coffee?' She led the way through to the cosy living room.

'That would be very nice.' He sat down in what was usually Rose's chair, staring into the fire, while Rachel made coffee and searched for some of Rose's shortbread. 'Is something wrong?' she asked anxiously as she put the tray down on a stool between them and poured the coffee.

'No. Well, yes.' He shifted in his chair. 'I've been talking to my father....'

'About my aunt?'

He nodded. 'Yes. He's been in touch with Archie Murdoch and it looks as if Rose will be in hospital for weeks, months probably.'

Rachel sipped her coffee slowly. 'Melanie will miss her.'

'We shall all miss Rose, but Melanie more than anyone. I'm afraid....' he sighed. 'I just don't know what to do about her.' He banged his cup down. 'What's the matter with the child? Why can't she be like other children? I've done everything I can think of. This speech therapy business is obviously a waste of time. . . .' He put his head in his hands. 'The answer, of course, is to send her to school.'

'Do that and she'll feel completely rejected.' Rachel curled both hands round her cup. 'As I see it, everyone loves Melanie but nobody wants her. She needs someone to spend time with her, helping her, doing things with her.' She made a gesture with her hands. 'Oh, I know Ben is very good, he talks to her a lot, but he isn't really helping her.' She looked up at Richard. 'What none of you seem to realise is all that's wrong with Melanie is that she's missing her mother. She needs loving, and showing she's loved.'

As soon as she had spoken the words Rachel could have bitten her tongue out. Seeing the agonised expression that crossed Richard's face she bent her head. 'I'm sorry. Forgive me, I shouldn't have said that.'

Richard shook his head. 'If only you knew. . . .' He seemed to pull himself together with an effort. 'Is there any more coffee?' he asked.

Rachel refilled his cup, her heart heavy. At this moment he looked so vulnerable she would have liked to put her arms round him and comfort him, to hold him close to her heart.

'What are you going to do now that Rose isn't here?' he asked cutting across her thoughts.

'Why, I'm not sure. I haven't really had time to decide.' She got up and went over to the window, looking out on the gathering dusk. 'I suppose I'll go back home. Rose is being well looked after. If she needs me when—if she comes out of hospital perhaps I could come back for a while. I have to go back and pick up the threads sometime.' She bowed her head as she spoke and her voice was low. But it was not the thought of going home that upset her, she realised that, it was the thought of leaving Richard Duncan behind. And he would barely notice that she had gone.

He got up from his chair and came and stood behind her, resting his hand on the window frame by her head.

'You could stay,' he said quietly. 'You could remain here as Melanie's governess—I don't like that word, but you know what I mean—win her confidence, teach her, help her,' his voice dropped, 'perhaps even grow to love her.'

Rachel was silent, conscious of the man standing so close behind her that if she moved her head it would rest on his shoulder. She held her breath, afraid to speak in case her emotions gave her away.

Richard moved away and went over to the table. 'Of course, it's what my father has always wanted, for Melanie to be educated at home, so it would please him if you agreed.' He sighed, adding as an after-thought, 'Goodness knows, I seem to do little enough to please him these days.' His tone became more businesslike. 'I'm sure we can come to an amicable agreement over salary etc. You would, of course, live at Kilfinan House.'

For a long time Rachel didn't speak. She stood watching the darkness gradually enveloping the mountains, her thoughts in a turmoil. She should say no. She should go home, leave this place that was so beautiful it was almost unreal, and this man who having asked her to stay, would only regard her presence as a sign of defeat—of having given in to his father over Melanie's education. To stay would be to invite heartbreak all over again.

'I'll stay,' she whispered, adding, 'For Melanie's sake.'

CHAPTER FOUR

RACHEL woke next morning with mixed feelings. She had agreed to move into Kilfinan House right away and begin looking after Melanie, but she couldn't help wondering if she was doing the right thing. To actually live under the same roof as Richard Duncan could only be to torture herself—exquisite torture though it might be—knowing he was there, aching to be held in his arms, while he was scarcely aware of her existence except as governess for his little daughter. Governess. She must keep reminding herself of that Victorian word, conjuring up, as it did, a picture of a nobody—neither servant nor master, belonging neither 'upstairs' nor 'downstairs'.

She packed a few things in a suitcase, the rest would be collected later, locked the door to Rose's cottage and walked up the drive to Kilfinan House. Richard was just about to leave. He was wearing a dark grey suit with a blue shirt and immaculately knotted striped tie. Rachel caught her breath. He looked incredibly handsome and smart.

'I have to go to Glasgow today, on business;' he said by way of explanation. He took her suitcase from her and as he bent his head she caught a faint hint of after-shave. 'But I've got time to take these up for you and show you your rooms before I go.' He led the way from the kitchen down a corridor and into a wide square parquet-floored hall, where two large carved oak chests, a suit of armour and several tapestry-covered chairs lined the walls. A grandfather clock with a friendly silver face stood at the first bend of the wide, thickly carpeted oak staircase. Rachel followed him up the stairs and along a corridor off to the left, lined either side with doors. There was a long stained-glass window at the end of the corridor.

'This is the wing we live in, as you probably know,' he explained. 'That's my father's study,' he indicated the first door on the right, 'and his bedroom next to it. My rooms are these, opposite. Then there are the bathrooms and guest rooms, Melanie's playroom, bed-room and bathroom.' Rachel recognised the three doors on the right that he pointed out from putting Melanie to bed the previous evening. 'Your bedroom and sitting room are these, opposite Melanie's rooms. I'm sure you won't mind sharing Melanie's bathroom.' He opened the last door on the left.

It was a sunny room, with windows on two walls, one looking out over the glen to the mountains beyond, the other looking on to the woods on the estate where Melanie loved to play, with, far in the distance, a thin grey ribbon which was the road to Ardenbeg. The room itself was furnished in blue and grey, with a grey carpet and deep blue dralon curtains and chair coverings. There were two comfortable armchairs, a small low table, portable television and radio, built-in bookshelves full of books and a long teak sideboard. An electric fire was built into a long row of fitments along one wall, which also incorporated cupboards and a cushioned fireside bench. It was a very comfort-able room. In one corner there was a connecting door to the bedroom.

This was furnished in a completely different style. The four-poster bed was draped in William Morris print to match the curtains. The walls and carpet were a plain, deep cream. The table beside the bed, the chest

of drawers and the kidney-shaped dressing table—also
draped in William Morris print—with its dainty triple
mirror, were all clearly very old, but well cared for.

'They're lovely rooms,' Rachel said warmly. 'I'm
sure I shall be very comfortable.'

'I hope you will.' Richard regarded her thoughtfully
for a moment, then said briskly, 'I daresay Rose has
already shown you over the rest of the house, so you'll
know your way about.' He went over to the window.
'You have a fine view over the glen. My windows have
this view, too. I never tire of it. Melanie's rooms and
my father's face the other way, towards the mountain.'
He turned away from the window, glancing at his
watch. 'I must go. I've a meeting at twelve and it's a
long drive to Glasgow. Melanie's away playing in the
woods. I did tell her you'd be coming but,' he sighed,
'I don't know whether she understood.'

'Don't worry, I'll explain to her,' said Rachel.

'Thank you.' He looked at his watch again. 'I must
go. If there's anything you want you must tell me. . . .'

'I'm sure there's everything I could possibly need
here.'

'I hope so.' He went to the door, then stopped and
turned back. 'My father rang Archie Murdoch again
this morning. Rose is quite comfortable and happy.'

'Oh, I'm so glad.'

'She was worried about you. My father said it re
lieved her to know you were coming here to live.'

'Oh.' Rachel didn't quite know what else to say. She
wished Richard would go, yet she wanted him to stay.

'I hope you'll be happy here.'

'I'm sure I shall.'

He looked at her for a moment as if he was going to
say something else, but a car horn sounded on the drive
below. 'That'll be Moira,' he said instead. 'She has some
shopping to do in Glasgow, so I'm giving her a lift.'

He left, and Rachel sat down in the nearest armchair, weak at the knees. If Richard Duncan was going to have this effect on her each time they met life was going to prove difficult. She must pull herself together and remember that Moira McLeod had laid claim to Richard, and if he married anyone it would be her, not Melanie's governess. She got up from her chair and went over to the window. Moira had parked her car and was just getting in beside Richard. She was wearing a beautifully cut blue trouser suit and her make-up was immaculate. As the car door closed and Richard drove off her tinkling laugh floated up to Rachel. Sadly, she turned away from the window and went to unpack her things.

When she had done this she went to look for Melanie. She was surprised to find as she stepped outside that the day, which had begun quite bright, had become overcast and thin drizzle was beginning to fall. Surely Melanie wouldn't be playing in the woods in such weather. Then she heard the sound of an axe from a nearby barn. Perhaps she was with Ben.

Ben was chopping logs with a rhythmic swinging movement which made it look deceptively easy. Melanie was playing with heaps of sawdust in a far corner. 'I was looking for Melanie,' said Rachel, pretending not to have seen her. 'I suppose you can't tell me where she is, Ben? You see, I've only just moved into Kilfinan House and I'm not sure where to find anything. I thought she might be able to help me. Nobody else seems to have time.' Rachel had decided on this approach after much thought.

Ben grinned, catching Rachel's idea. 'No, I've not seen her, Rachel, but if you'll wait a wee while till I finish these logs I'll be happy to come round with you myself.'

Immediately there was a scuffling noise from the

corner and Melanie came and slipped her hand into Rachel's.

'Oh, *there* you are. I was looking all over for you.' Rachel feigned surprise. 'Well, there are lots of things I need to know about. Will you help me?'

Melanie nodded. She neither smiled nor lifted her eyes. It was going to be a long, slow business getting through to the little girl, Rachel realised, but, feeling the warm little hand in her own, she had no doubt that she would win in the end.

The day passed quickly. When Melanie had taken her to see everything in the house that Rachel could think of they went to Melanie's playroom and did jigsaws and cut out pictures. Rachel was saddened to see the brand-new, expensive toys that lined the room, mostly unused—bought, she guessed, mostly by Alistair as a sop to his conscience.

The rain was coming down in torrents by now and the top of the mountain was completely hidden in the thick accompanying mist. This was something that never ceased to amaze Rachel; how a huge solid bulk that was a mountain could seem to disappear so utterly and completely, just as if it had been spirited away.

She voiced these thoughts to Melanie. All day long she had talked to the child, telling her about her home in Suffolk, about the children she had taught and the funny things they did; she told her about Rose, that she had had an accident and been taken to hospital but that they hoped she would be better before long. Occasionally she threw in a question, hoping that perhaps in an unguarded moment Melanie might forget herself and answer. But she didn't. A nod or brief shake of the head was the only indication that she had even heard what had been said to her.

Patience, Rachel reminded herself as she tucked the

little girl into bed and kissed her goodnight. Melanie must be given time.

It was arranged that Rachel should eat her evening meal with Alistair and Richard after Melanie was in bed, so she changed the maroon trousers and blue sweater that she had been wearing all day for a dress of pale green and went down to the dining room. Alistair was there, alone. He was wearing a tweed suit and turtle-neck sweater.

'Richard's not back yet. Don't know what's kept him. He said he'd be back for dinner,' he said in his abrupt manner, adding, 'We don't dress for dinner when we're by ourselves, but I'm pleased to see you're wearing a dress. Pity to cover up a pair of shapely legs with trousers. Sherry, lassie?'

'Please.' Rachel couldn't help smiling. Alistair Duncan was blunt and direct, you felt you knew where you stood with him.

'Celia wore trousers sometimes. Not always, though. Not always. She knew I liked to see her in a dress. She knew how to dress, too, did Celia.'

'You must miss her,' Rachel prompted.

He nodded. 'Yes. She was a bonny lass.' He didn't speak of her further but it was obvious from his tone that he had been fond of his daughter-in-law.

Over dinner, cooked by one of the women who came in from the clachan, Alistair talked about Rose. His concern for her went far beyond that of an employer towards his employee, he spoke of her as a long-standing and very dear friend.

The meal was dull and not particularly well cooked, but Alistair didn't seem to notice and when it was over he excused himself and went to his study. Rachel went up to her sitting room, first looking in at Melanie.

She was fast asleep, clutching an old teddy, but instead of the relaxed features of a normal healthy child, her face wore a frown and her whole body was tense. Rachel stood looking down at her for a long time. If only she could find a way through the barrier of silence that engulfed Melanie!

She went thoughtfully to her room and turned on the radio to drown the sound of the rain lashing down. Melanie, it seemed, had never been a talkative child, but it was not until her mother's death that she had ceased talking altogether. Rachel frowned. She knew so little about Celia, yet everything she had heard pointed to her having been a remarkable woman. What little Alistair had said of her had been with a note of affection, Ben had clearly been more than half in love with her, and Richard had still not got over losing her, hiding his broken heart at times under a veneer of suave cynicism. Yet there was no clue to her actual character; only Rose had given a hint when she said, 'Richard's wife hated it here. She missed the social life she had been used to.' Yet she had given it up to marry Richard and bury herself in the country with him. She must have been very much in love—a feeling Rachel didn't find it hard to understand.

At ten o'clock Rachel still had not heard the sound of Richard's car on the drive. Several times during the evening she looked out of the window, thinking she heard it, but each time she had been mistaken. She told herself that he was probably spending the evening at the farm with Moira after their day in Glasgow, or perhaps they had gone to dinner and the theatre there. None of these alternatives gave her any comfort at all, in fact she found that there was an uncomfortable feeling, not unlike jealousy, gnawing inside her. It's nothing to do with me what Richard Duncan does, she told herself sternly, nor who he is with. I'm only here to look after his daughter.

She went to bed. She had never before slept in a four-poster bed and she found it a luxurious feeling. All the same she couldn't sleep and at eleven she went downstairs to make herself a milky drink in the hope that it would help her to sleep.

She found milk in the fridge and when she had warmed it she put it in a mug taken from a hook on the dresser. She was about to carry it up to her room when she heard the front door bang and a few seconds later Richard strode into the kitchen, his face like a thundercloud. He was wearing yellow oilskins, but even so he was soaked to the skin and looked frozen with cold.

'Car broke down the other side of Ardenbeg,' he said briefly, 'miles from anywhere. And not another car passed me. I've had to walk twelve miles. Of all the filthy nights for this to happen!'

'Why didn't you phone for help?' Rachel asked.

'Lines are down. I tried.'

Rachel put her tray down on the table in order to help him off with his oilskins. 'Good thing I always keep these in the car,' he said as he struggled out of them. 'Don't pull there, get hold of the sleeve.' He put his arm out impatiently. 'That's better. God, I could do with a drink, but I must get some dry clothes on first.'

'But what about Moira?' Rachel gave a final tug. He had made her nearly as wet as he was himself, the front of her housecoat was saturated. 'You can't leave her stranded in a broken-down car on a night like this.'

He looked blank for a moment. 'Moira? Oh, she's spending the night with friends. I only gave her a lift into Glasgow, I don't know what she was doing after that, except that she wasn't coming back tonight. Ugh!' He took off his shoes; they were full of water. 'I'm going upstairs to change.'

'Would you like me to make you a drink?' Rachel asked.

'Please. The Scotch is on the sideboard in the dining room, and I'd like a large one. On second thoughts bring the decanter. I'll be in my study, it's probably warmer there than it is down here.' He went off, muttering to himself.

Rachel, her milky drink forgotten, collected the whisky decanter from the dining room and took it to Richard's study, first slipping back to her own rooms to change from her wet housecoat to a long woollen skirt and lambswool sweater because she was beginning to feel chilled.

Richard's study was not a big room although the high ceiling gave an illusion of space. The walls were lined with books and charts and the flat-topped desk by the window was littered with papers. Two leather-covered armchairs flanked the electric fire, which Rachel was glad to switch on, putting the tray holding the decanter and glass on a low table beside it. Then she poured a generous drink for Richard.

'Didn't you bring a glass for yourself?' He came in, wearing sandals, jeans and a dark green sweater, towelling his hair dry as he came. 'Never mind, it doesn't matter, I think there are some here.' He went over to a small corner cupboard hanging on the wall and took out a tumbler, handing it to her. Then running a comb through his hair he threw himself into the nearest armchair and took a gulp of his drink. 'Ah, that's better. I feel a little more human now.' He closed his eyes. 'I've had one hell of a day in Glasgow and the car breaking down just about clinched everything.'

Rachel perched on the arm of the other chair, sipped her drink and said nothing.

After a moment he opened his eyes. 'Have you made any progress with Melanie?' he asked. His voice had a sharp edge to it.

Rachel was taken slightly aback at his tone. 'I've only

been with her a day,' she reminded him. 'I can't work miracles.'

'No, of course not.' He poured himself another drink. 'I'm still not convinced that this is the right thing for the child, although my father, naturally, is happy about it. I think school is what she needs. Plenty of discipline....'

'Security is what Melanie needs more than anything,' Rachel found herself saying vehemently.

'Nonsense. She's secure enough. She's lived here all her life; she knows every inch of the house and grounds. What better security could she have? No, it's discipline she needs. She's spoiled, that's the trouble.' He drained his glass and put it down on the tray. 'My father's the culprit, of course. You must have seen all those expensive toys in the playroom. He buys her all these things, but she never plays with them, she's simply not interested. She'd rather be running wild in the woods, or out with Ben. It's not good for her. As I see it, school's the only answer.'

'Then why don't you send her?' Rachel was becoming faintly irritated by his tone.

'Because, to put it bluntly, I can't afford to.' He looked up at her, still perched on the arm of her chair, and his mouth hardened. 'If you'll spare a moment and sit in that chair properly I'll tell you why.'

Obediently, she slid into the seat of the chair.

He sat forward. 'My father, as you've no doubt been able to reason for yourself, is a rich man,' he said. 'This house ... the grounds ... outlying farms....' he spread his hands. 'Also, you will have been able to see for yourself that he is neither too old nor too infirm to run the Estate. In fact, everything runs very smoothly under his direction and he's very happy doing it.' He leaned back in his chair. 'So where does that leave me?'

'As his assistant?' Rachel suggested.

'Oh, yes, he'd like that. In fact, he'd like that more than anything,' Richard said bitterly. 'But I shouldn't. If I take over this estate it has to be on *my* terms. I would want to run it *my* way, not his. There are several areas where we don't agree even now, and it would be even worse if we were actually working together.' He shook his head. 'No, until he retires I'll have nothing to do with running this estate; that's why I started my own business at Ardenbeg. It's quite different, quite set apart from anything here, and eventually it should make me quite a respectable living. But, even more important than that, it's completely mine. I run it the way *I* choose, I've built it up from nothing with no help, financial or otherwise, from anyone. Unfortunately, up to the moment, although it's ticking over quite satisfactorily, the profits haven't been sufficient to pay the fees of the school I have in mind for my daughter. Now, this is one area where I would be prepared to accept help from my father, but it is also, sadly, the one area where he is not willing to give it, simply because he doesn't want Melanie to be sent away to school.' He got up from his chair and stood with his back to the electric fire. 'Call it blackmail if you like, but he has said he will pay for her to go to school if I come into his business. And this I refuse to do, even for Melanie, because I know what problems it would cause.'

'And you're trying to tell me that Melanie has security,' Rachel breathed.

'She has. All this is over her head. It doesn't directly concern her at all.'

'That's what *you* think. Do you imagine she doesn't sense the antagonism between you and your father? She may not understand it, but she'll know it's there *and* that she's the cause of it. You're *using* her, both of you, to get your own way.'

Richard shook his head coolly. 'You're wrong. My father is quite happy with the way things are. He'd like me back in the running of the Estate, but he's in no desperate hurry. He doesn't want Melanie to be sent to school, although he would finance this as a ...' his lip curled sardonically, '... "reward" to me. No, by and large he's got what he wants, which is a governess for her.' He gazed at Rachel and his eyes were cold. 'Believe me, *I'm* the one who isn't happy about that, but at the moment there's nothing I can do about it.'

Rachel felt her colour rising in humiliation. She put her glass down carefully on the tray and stood up. This was the side of Richard Duncan that she had encountered on their first meeting, on the journey to Glencarrick from Dunglevin; it showed a cold, ruthless man who had no feelings for others. The real Richard Duncan.

She went over to the door. 'My concern is with your daughter,' she said quietly, although she was seething with rage inside. 'The difficulties between you and your father have nothing whatever to do with me. I'm here to help Melanie and to teach her what I can, and this I shall do to the best of my ability as long as I am required here.' She went out, not waiting for him to reply, closing the door carefully behind her. At least now she knew exactly where she stood with Richard Duncan. Not only was she in the lowly position of being a governess to his child, but an unwelcome one at that. Could there be anything more degrading?

Back in her room she undressed, climbed into the four-poster bed and on her first night under the roof of Kilfinan House cried herself to sleep.

CHAPTER FIVE

The next morning Rachel woke early. The day was fine and the trees, saturated after the previous night's rain, seemed to drip diamonds in the bright sunlight. She got up and dressed herself in a blue gingham dress and went to rouse Melanie. The little girl was already awake and out of bed sitting on the window seat and staring out of the window.

'Time to get dressed, Melanie,' Rachel greeted her. Melanie responded by turning her head and gazing at Rachel. Then she studied her shorts and T-shirt, neatly folded on the chair by her bed.

'Come along, now. We haven't all day to waste.' Rachel spoke kindly but firmly.

Melanie slid from her perch and went to the chest of drawers beside her bed, where she rummaged for a few moments before selecting a dress of identical gingham to Rachel's.

'That's nice,' Rachel commented. 'It's just like mine.'

A pleased expression crossed Melanie's face—it could hardly be called a smile—and she smoothed the dress carefully as she put it on.

They spent the morning at the playroom table, where Rachel tried to assess the little girl's capabilities. She had decided that mornings should be set aside for 'school' at first, gradually increasing the time as Melanie progressed. It was hard work. Melanie refused to draw, refused even to hold a pencil, and at last Rachel resorted to a bag of old building bricks she found in a cupboard, counting them into piles and labelling them with the appropriate numbers. By the end of the morning she was more exhausted than she would have thought possible and depressed because she had failed to make any headway at all. It was like trying to teach a brick wall, she reflected, packing the building bricks back into their bag while Melanie looked on, not even offering to hold the bag open for her.

Before going in to lunch Rachel slipped outside for a breath of fresh air. Ben was just on his way back to the barn.

'It's my afternoon off today,' he said. 'And a lovely day at that. Would you and Melanie like to come with me for a picnic at Eilean Dorcha?'

Rachel frowned, puzzled. 'Eilean Dorcha?' she repeated.

'The little island by the lighthouse that I showed you the other day. Don't you remember?'

'Oh, yes. But I didn't know that was what it was called. At least, if you told me I'd forgotten.' Rachel smiled. 'I'd love to go there for a picnic.'

'Good. I'll see you about two o'clock, then.'

After lunch Rachel packed a picnic, changed into jeans and a check shirt and made sure Melanie did the same. She was just stowing the picnic in the Mini when Ben arrived and they set off.

It was a glorious day. The sun was brilliant and there was not a cloud to be seen. The mountains all around stood green and brown, sharply contoured against the bright blue sky. Here and there a waterfall on the mountainside glistened in the brightness, for all the world like a giant snail tracking down the mountainside.

Rachel drove, at Ben's insistence, and he sat beside her, with Melanie bouncing in the back, excited to be going out with her beloved Ben. They drove straight through Ardenbeg and took the road to Dunglevin, Ben telling her that the road to the lighthouse would branch off this road about a mile out of the town. He had hardly said this when Melanie, realising they were on the Dunglevin road, suddenly flung her arms round Ben's neck, nearly choking him. She was trembling with fear and her face was like parchment.

'Hey, hey, little one, what's wrong?' Ben extricated himself with difficulty from Melanie's clasp. 'What's frightened you?' He gazed all around him. 'Can you see what's scared her, Rachel?' he asked.

'No. I can't see anything at all.' Rachel was puzzled. She couldn't understand it. What could have struck such terror into the child?

Once out of Ardenbeg the houses had thinned and on one side of the road, beyond a narrow stretch of marshland, lay the loch, while on the other rose the sheer side of the mountain. It was very strange.

She drove on, with Ben making soothing noises to calm Melanie, until she came to the turning on to the lower coast road. Immediately, Melanie relaxed. She was still deathly pale, but her terror seemed to subside. Rachel frowned. What could strike such terror into the child at the thought of going to Dunglevin? It could only have been that that frightened her, because as soon as they turned off the Dunglevin road her fear had subsided. Surely the speech therapist wasn't such a dragon!

The road followed very roughly the shore of the loch, gradually degenerating into little more than a cart track through the undergrowth. Rachel was just beginning to wonder if in fact they had come too far or somehow missed the way when the track widened into a clearing and there was the island, Eilean Dorcha, less than a quarter of a mile away, dark green against the blue of the loch.

They all got out of the car. There seemed to be a tiny natural harbour here and two or three boats were moored between the island and the mainland, which seemed to curve round in a promontory thick with trees and bushes, ending in a rocky tip on which the lighthouse stood. Taking the picnic basket and a rug they found their way through the undergrowth to the lighthouse. It was tiny, little more than fifteen feet high and quite derelict. Rachel kicked off her sandals and rolled up her jeans to her knees. Melanie watched her for a moment and then followed suit; Ben was already wearing shorts. Then for an hour or more the three of them clambered over the rocks, watching the fishes dart in the clear, deep water, exploring the rock pools and watching tiny crabs scuttle for cover. Rachel and Ben talked encouragingly to Melanie all the while and soon the colour returned to her cheeks. Once or twice the little girl's face darkened with jealousy when Ben gave Rachel a helping hand over difficult rocks, but soon she forgot this in her absorption.

They ate their picnic sitting on the rocks, Ben leaning his back against the rock on which Rachel was sitting, Melanie close beside him. He was very good with the little girl, Rachel observed; he talked to her all the time, but he never seemed to expect, indeed, he never encouraged her to talk back. Rachel couldn't help wondering why her aunt was so antagonistic towards Ben.

When they had finished eating Melanie went off by herself to explore the lighthouse; clearly she had come to realise that Rachel was no threat to her friendship with Ben. Rachel packed the basket with Ben looking on.

'Do you like it in these parts, Rachel?' he asked, idly tossing a stone into the water.

'Very much.' She paused in the act of packing the last item. 'It's all so quiet and peaceful.'

'You're looking very much better.' Ben looked up at her from the rock on which he was sitting and the expression in his eyes made her blush. 'I'm sorry about Rose's accident, but I'm glad it's given you an excuse to stay on here.'

She stood up quickly. 'Where's Melanie? I'm not sure that it's good for her to go off on her own. She could easily get lost and she can't call us to let us know where she is.' She spoke quickly to cover her embarrassment.

Ben stood up, too. As he stood on a rock below her his face was on a level with hers. He leaned forward and kissed her lightly, full on the lips. 'That's to say thank you for a pleasant afternoon,' he said softly.

It was nothing more than a friendly kiss, but Rachel felt uneasy, particularly as, looking over his shoulder, she saw, just passing the island, a fishing boat, the *Celia*, with a tall dark man at the wheel. Wasn't *Celia* the name of Richard's boat? And wasn't the man at the wheel Richard himself?

Somehow, for Rachel, all the brightness had gone out of the day.

A few days later Alistair surprised Rachel by saying at the breakfast table, 'I shall be going into Dunglevin this afternoon to visit Rose. If you'd care to come with me you're very welcome. No doubt Ben will be happy to look after Melanie for a few hours.'

'Thank you, I'd like to come,' Rachel replied.

Alistair got up from the table and left, absent-mindedly patting Melanie's head as he passed her chair. Rachel was puzzled. He hadn't even spoken to his granddaughter, yet Richard insisted that he was opposed to her being sent away to school. But if he always took as little notice of her as that what possible difference could it make to him whether she was in the house or not?

As always Rachel and Melanie spent the morning at the playroom table. The child was intelligent, Rachel had no doubt on that score. But it was just as if the child had put a shutter up between herself and the rest of the world and so far Rachel could find no chink in it.

Richard and Alistair were both at lunch, prepared by a woman from the clachan, Mrs Munroe, who, it seemed, would be acting as cook in Rose's absence.

'How can I deputise for you? I know nothing whatever about the soil on Isaac's Farm,' Richard was saying as Rachel entered the dining room with Melanie. 'Why can't Ben do it?'

'Because it's not Ben's job.' Alistair helped himself to vegetables. 'I'd forgotten the soil analysis man was coming this afternoon when I arranged to take Rachel to see Rose in hospital. Quite forgotten. But if you'd deputise for me. . . .'

'I have my own business to run. I'm taking a fishing party round Lamont Point this afternoon. In any case, I know absolutely nothing about soil analysis.' Richard shook open his napkin and picked up his knife and fork, putting an end to the discussion. 'But why can't Rachel go alone?' he asked as an afterthought. 'She drives the Mini. And the road to Dunglevin is clearly marked. She's not likely to miss her way.'

'Would you do that, lassie?' Alistair asked anxiously. 'I'd not want to disappoint Rose, but we've been waiting for this analysis laddie for months, I'd not want to miss him, either.'

'Yes, of course.' Rachel smiled at Alistair. At that moment she felt a surge of pity for him at Richard's complete indifference and lack of co-operation. It must be a sad disappointment to the older man.

As for Richard, he ate his lunch, and with barely an apology excused himself and left, saying he had to prepare the boat for the afternoon trip.

After lunch Rachel took Melanie to find Ben, who was stacking logs in a far corner of the barn.

'She'll be happy enough here with me,' Ben smiled. 'I'll see she comes to no harm.'

Rachel found the drive to Dunglevin interesting. She drove through Ardenbeg and over the high road by the loch, then the road wound sometimes between the mountains, sometimes over them. The scenery was breathtaking in its grandeur, but nowhere could it match the view Ben had shown her from the vantage point on the scenic road above the loch and she resolved to stop there again on the way home. The hospital, directions for which Alistair had given her most explicitly, was on the far side of Dunglevin and she had no difficulty whatsoever in finding it.

Rose was lying flat on her back. She insisted that as long as she remained still she was in no pain and although her face was pale she was losing the lines of strain and tiredness. Rachel saw, with something of a shock, that her aunt had been a striking-looking woman in her younger days.

Inevitably, it was not long before the conversation turned to Melanie.

'I'm glad you're going to look after her, my girl,' Rose said, 'but are you sure that it's the right thing for you to do?' Her eyes searched her niece's face. 'After all, you only came here for a holiday. Will you not be wanting to get back to your own home? In fact,' she put a hand up to Rachel's arm, 'are you sure you're not using this as an excuse *not* to go home and face things?'

Rachel was silent for a long time. She could think of Keith and the life they would have had together quite dispassionately now. The time they had had together would always be a valuable part of her life, but she had come to terms with her loss, her life had moved on. The fact that she had become infatuated by Richard Duncan was surely proof of that. And it *was* only infatuation, she told herself sternly. The tempestuous feelings that Richard aroused in her bore no resemblance to the steady, warm glow of affection she had shared with Keith.

She turned to her aunt. 'I love it here in Scotland,' she said, simply. 'But I'm not running away from life by staying here, please don't think that.'

Rose nodded contentedly. 'It's good to have you near me. It'll be good for Melanie, too. I've tried....' She sighed. 'She needs affection, that's half the trouble. It's something I've never been very good at showing, somehow. I'm short with her when I know I shouldn't be, I realise that.'

'It's understandable. She's not an easy child to deal with.'

'That's no excuse. I've failed her. Poor lamb, she needs someone to show her they love her in a way I could never bring myself to do. Lying here with time on my hands and looking back over the years I can see that that's what's wrong with her. She's starved of affection.'

'Alistair's fond of her, in his way,' Rachel said thoughtfully.

'Yes, he's prepared to give her anything in the world —except his time.'

'And Richard. Surely he ....'

'Richard can never accept that he could have fathered a less than perfect child. Melanie embarrasses him,' Rose said shrewdly. 'He simply doesn't know how to treat her.'

'She certainly seems happiest when she's with Ben,' Rachel mused. 'And he never minds having her with him.'

'That's what worries me more than anything. Melanie should never be allowed to spend so much time with Ben.' Rose spoke vehemently. 'Oh, don't misunderstand me. He would never let any harm come to her, he's very fond of her, I'm sure of that. But....'

'You think she's substituting Ben for her mother in some way? Looking to him for affection she had from Celia?'

Rose snorted. 'She never *had* any affection from her mother. Celia didn't want her and took no interest in her when she'd got her. All *she* thought about was having a good time. The different men....' Suddenly she sighed. 'Oh, what's the use? It's all in the past, why rake it up? Best let it lie forgotten.' She closed her eyes wearily. 'It was good of you to come and see me, my girl. You'll come again, won't you?'

'Of course I will.' Rachel leaned over and kissed her aunt. 'Often.'

She left Rose then, seeing how the visit had tired her, and took the opportunity to explore the town of Dunglevin a little, since there was no immediate urgency for her to return to Glencarrick, and go over in her mind what Rose had told her. She made a few leisurely purchases and had a look at the ruined castle on the hill before having tea at a quiet little teashop where the waitress had a motherly face and a soft Scottish burr as she offered, 'Scones or teacakes?'

After that she spent a while watching the steamers, remembering how, not so long ago, she had been one of the crowd spilling off the boat on to the pier. That day, with its depressing torrential rain, seemed very distant now. She thought of the people she had met and with whose lives her own had become linked; kind, friendly Ben. What could Rose possibly find to dislike in him? And Celia? What could her aunt have meant? She seemed to have been implying that Richard's wife was nothing more than a playgirl, out for a good time. Yet how could that be true? Everyone else spoke highly of Celia, and she would surely never have buried herself at Glencarrick if it were true because from what Rachel had seen of the night-life of the district there was little to attract a good-time girl. In fact, as far as she could see the only eligible bachelor for miles was Ben.

She frowned. Ben had plainly been more than half in love with Richard's wife, that was obvious from the way he spoke about her.... But no, it wasn't possible. Aunt Rose must be imagining things, or the fall had damaged more than her back. Richard Duncan was not a man to have the wool pulled over his eyes. He had clearly idolised his wife. Why, he had named his boat after her and even now, two years after her death, he still found it painful to speak of her. A man like Richard Duncan would never have such regard for an unfaithful wife. Rachel shook her head in perplexity. Maybe the drugs they were giving Rose were having an hallucinatory effect. It was the only explanation.

She looked at her watch. It was past six, time to be heading home if she wanted to see Melanie bathed and into bed. That was one thing Rose had been right about, the child needed someone she could rely on for

love, and that was a role Rachel would have no difficulty in filling. She was becoming very fond of Melanie.

She collected her car from the car park and began
the hour-long journey back to Glencarrick. After a day
of warm sunshine there was a chill nip now in the air
and Rachel was glad she had brought a warm suede
jacket with her.

She was little more than halfway on the journey
home when she noticed the noise. It was a peculiar
knocking sound, coming spasmodically from somewhere
in the bowels of the car. She bit her lip, hoping there
was nothing wrong with the mechanics of the car, this
was something she was completely ignorant about. She
was very conscious that Dunglevin was fifteen miles
behind her and also that she had at least another
twelve to go before reaching Ardenbeg.

She pulled into a lay-by to investigate and as she did
so the engine died with nothing more than a gentle
splutter. In some alarm she tried to re-start the car, but
without success. It was completely dead. It was then
that she noticed the petrol gauge. It registered zero.

With a groan of despair she put her head down on the
steering wheel. Of all the feather-brained, stupid things
to do—to run out of petrol on roads as lonely and
isolated as these! Why, oh, why hadn't she checked?
She clenched her fists and brought them down on to the
dashboard in furious frustration, cursing herself for her
lack of foresight. When at last she began to think con-
structively again she realised that there was only one
thing she could do. She would have to wait and flag
down the next passing car.

She got out of the Mini. Parked as it was high on a
slope she could see the road stretching empty in both
directions for several miles. There was not even a farmhouse in view, nor the welcome tell-tale red of a tele-

phone kiosk. She began to walk up and down with nothing but the odd ruminating sheep for company.

After half an hour, during which it became progressively colder, she realised the futility of simply waiting to be rescued. This was simply not going to happen. There was no alternative but to walk the twelve miles into Ardenbeg to find a garage and telephone Kilfinan House for help. Rachel pulled the grey suede jacket round her a little more closely, slung her bag over her shoulder and set off, glad that the sandals she was wearing were fairly flat and very comfortable. She did wish, however, that she had chosen to wear jeans instead of a full-skirted print dress.

As she walked the grandeur and beauty of the mountains gradually began to take on for her a slightly sinister and ominous aspect. It was the vastness and complete silence of it all that made her aware how tiny and insignificant one small human being was against this huge backdrop of nature. It made her feel very alone and just a little frightened.

She hurried on. She seemed to have been walking for ages, but looking back the way she had come she found the Mini still clearly in view, high on the hillside. Then, ahead of her, far in the distance, hardly bigger than an ant crawling along, she saw another car. With almost a sob of relief she watched it approach, often, when it became hidden by a fold in the contour of the road, fearing that it had turned off down some unseen cart-track. But then it would appear again, looming larger and larger until at last she could see, her relief turning almost into dismay, that it was Richard Duncan at the wheel, and his face was like thunder.

He pulled up with a jerk beside her and got out.

'What in heaven's name do you think you're doing?

You should have been back hours ago. Where's your car?' he barked.

Rachel pushed a strand of hair wearily back from her face. 'It's up there.' She pointed to where the Mini, its windscreen glinting in the last rays of the setting sun, was perched on the side of the mountain in its lay-by.

'Oh, has it broken down? That's tough luck.' He looked down at her, his face immediately full of concern. 'My goodness, you've walked quite a way, too. What's gone wrong with it, do you know?'

'Nothing,' She bit her lip. 'I've run out of petrol, that's all.'

'Oh, really!' He made a gesture of impatience. 'I would have thought you'd have had enough sense to keep a full tank. You must know how isolated these roads are. Of all the stupid, incompetent....' He got back into his car, still muttering and opened the passenger door for her. 'Get in. We'll have to fetch some from Ardenbeg.' He started the motor as she settled herself beside him, pausing before driving off. 'Here,' he said, rummaging behind him among the boots and fishing gear that littered the back of the car and finding his anorak. 'Put this round you, you look half frozen.' He placed it over her shoulders and pulled it round her as if she were a child. 'You must watch your petrol gauge,' he said, more gently. 'It's easy to travel for hours without coming to a petrol station— in fact, without passing another car—on these roads.' His eyes held hers for a moment and a half smile flickered across his face. Then it was gone, he turned the car expertly on the narrow road and they sped off the way he had come. 'I should have thought,' he added, his eyes on the road, 'that even you would have realised that.'

Rachel shrank a little in her seat. 'Even you.' That obviously summed up Richard Duncan's opinion of her; inadequate, thoughtless, stupid. Why was he never around when she was acting capably and intelligently? She glanced at his hands, square and firm on the steering wheel, then at his face, his jaw set granite-hard at the time he was wasting on her behalf. *He* would never do anything without due thought and preparation.

'Is Melanie all right?' she ventured.

'Mrs Munroe put her to bed—eventually. But it was quite a struggle. The child was far from happy at having a strange person to deal with.' His tone was not exactly accusing, but it made Rachel feel guilty, nevertheless, at not being there to settle her charge for the night. 'You could have put her to bed yourself,' she said tartly.

'I was not there. I didn't arrive home until half past seven and came straight out again to look for you.'

'Oh.' Rachel didn't quite know what else to say. They travelled the rest of the way in silence.

At Ardenbeg Richard went to the only garage, where he was obviously well-known, and bought petrol in a can. Then he drove at breakneck speed back to Rachel's abandoned Mini.

'I just hope this will have taught you a lesson,' he said as he emptied the can into her petrol tank. 'You've more than enough here to get you home, but make sure you fill up before you take the car out again. It was just fortunate that I knew where to come and look for you' He threw the empty can back into the boot of his car and wiped his hands on a piece of rag. He was still wearing jeans and his thick fisherman's sweater, although he had changed his heavy sea-boots for shoes. Perched rakishly on the back of his head was a cheese-cutter sailing cap.

'It was very kind of you,' Rachel said inadequately.

He finished cleaning his hands and got into his car. 'Right. I'll lead, you follow,' he said, slamming the door.

Rachel started the Mini. She knew she couldn't hope to keep up with Richard's powerful car and she had no intention of trying. But, to her surprise, he matched his speed to hers, and she knew that she was never out of range of his rear-view mirror. That, she told herself, was how little he felt he could trust her. It was humiliating.

Back at Kilfinan House he parked his car just ahead of her and came back to open her door for her.

'Thank you for coming to my rescue,' she said gratefully. 'Goodness knows what time I should have arrived home if you hadn't come.' She climbed out of the car as she spoke and found herself standing very close to him. He made no attempt to move, but stood looking down at her.

'I think,' he said slowly, 'I'm entitled to a little more than a mere thank you. I noticed the other day at Eilean Dorcha that you were behaving in quite a friendly way, to say the least, towards Ben Carson. What's good for him can't be bad for me, I think.' Swiftly, he bent his head and caught her to him, almost crushing her with the strength of his arms as his mouth came down on hers. For a moment she was powerless to move, then the implication of his words hit her and gave her an almost superhuman strength. She twisted her face away from his and broke from his grasp. Then, looking up at him, her face white with rage, she brought up her hand and dealt him a stinging blow on the cheek.

'How dare you!' she said, her voice low with fury. 'Perhaps you'll remember in future that I'm employed here as governess,' she gave the word its full emphasis, 'and that's all. It does not give you the right to take liberties of any other kind with me. I'll thank you not to forget this.'

She walked off, her head held high, hoping he couldn't see that she was trembling from head to foot, whether from rage or the effects of his embrace even she couldn't tell.

Richard watched her go, his hand held to his smarting cheek.

CHAPTER SIX

MELANIE woke Rachel next morning by bouncing on her bed. At first Rachel thought the child was cross with her for not being there at bedtime the previous night, but then she saw that Melanie was grinning with delight and excitement and obviously in very high spirits.

'Just wait a minute,' Rachel protested laughingly as Melanie attempted to drag her out of bed. She looked at her watch. 'My goodness, it's barely seven o'clock, we don't have to get up yet, do we?'

Melanie's face fell. She looked down at herself. She was fully dressed in clean shorts and a pretty blouse; she had washed and combed her hair, and Rachel could even detect a faint odour of toothpaste. All without a single reminder! There must be something extra special about today. Rachel tried to guess.

'It's your birthday!' She knew it couldn't be that, Melanie's birthday wasn't until the autumn.

Melanie shook her head, wriggling with excitement, obviously enjoying the game enormously.

Rachel tried to think what other treat the little girl might have in store and realised with something of a shock that Melanie's life contained little that a normal child would find exciting.

'All right, dear, you win. I'll get up and see what it is you want to show me.' Rachel struggled up in bed. 'Give me ten minutes.' She took Melanie's wrist and pointed to the hands on her watch. 'At half past seven the hands will be ... there ... and you can come back. Do you understand?'

Melanie nodded happily and skipped off. Rachel slid out of bed and began to dress. Soon she would have to face Richard at the breakfast table. After the way they had parted last night the encounter was not going to be easy. She sighed. She had so often dreamed of being in his arms, but not like that. No, never like that. But at least it had cured her infatuation. The only feeling she had now for Richard Duncan was cold disgust.

Melanie was back at seven-thirty on the dot. She must have been sitting outside watching the hands of her watch go round. Excitedly, she took Rachel's hand and led her downstairs and out of the house. The morning was bright and the grass dewy underfoot as Melanie skipped beside her over to the barn, where she flung open the big door.

The barn was gloomy after the brightness outside, but shafts of sunlight through the openings in the brickwork that served as windows picked out heaps of logs littering the floor. Rachel frowned. It was unlike Ben to leave such a mess, he was normally a very tidy man in his work.

Melanie was jumping up and down in a frenzy by this time and, tugging at Rachel's hand, she pulled her over to the logs. Suddenly Rachel could see what all the fuss was about. The logs were, she could now see, carefully placed in heaps and each heap was carefully numbered, the number having been drawn with a stick in the sawdust.

Rachel went from heap to heap. Six logs with a six beside them, one log a long one, eight logs a wobbly eight, the nine was the wrong way round but there were nine logs beside it.

'Did Ben help you, Melanie?' Rachel asked, amazed. Beaming, Melanie shook her head vigorously and pointed to herself, nearly bursting with pride and achievement.

Rachel knelt down and took the little girl in her arms. 'You clever girl, you remembered what I showed you. That's wonderful! Let's find Daddy and show him, shall we?'

For a moment the little figure stiffened, then Melanie relaxed and nodded happily.

Richard was just leaving the house as the two of them ran across from the barn.

'Come and see what Melanie's been doing,' Rachel called. Almost as excited as Melanie, she had no idea what an attractive picture she presented, in a simple flowered smock, her eyes sparkling and her face slightly flushed. Melanie hung back a little, but Richard smiled at her.

'Well, what have you been up to, then?' he asked, a trifle heartily.

Melanie grinned shyly and Rachel led the way to the barn. She could sense an awkwardness between Richard and his daughter and this saddened her. If he was not at ease with the little girl how could he hope to help her?

In the barn Rachel explained how previously she had counted and labelled building bricks in the playroom for Melanie.

'She didn't seem to be paying any attention at all to what I was doing,' said Rachel. 'In fact, I thought I was wasting my time.' She smiled and spread her hands, 'but obviously she *was* taking notice. She's got them all correct, too. Isn't it wonderful?'

'It's a beginning,' Richard said cautiously. 'But no doubt Ben helped her.'

'She says not.'

'Says?' He turned to her sharply.

'I'm sorry. I meant she shook her head with some violence when I asked her if he did. Ben didn't help you, did he, Melanie?'

Melanie shook her head vehemently. She was so obviously pleased with her achievement that it was impossible not to believe her.

Rachel bent down and kissed her. 'I think you're a clever girl and we're proud of you. Aren't we?' She looked up at Richard for confirmation.

'Yes. It's very good.' He made no attempt to embrace his little daughter, nor even to pat her head. But Melanie didn't seem to notice. She skipped out of the barn and back to the house, her thick black hair, so like her father's, bobbing as she ran.

Richard perched himself on the edge of a nearby sawing horse, in a beam of sunlight, his hands in the pockets of his jeans. 'You're beginning to make headway, then?' he asked.

'Shall we say we've discovered the first chink of light,' Rachel answered, matching his earlier caution. She traced a pattern in the sawdust with the toe of her sandal. Suddenly she looked up and was surprised to find Richard's eyes on her.

'You certainly seem to understand her,' he said thoughtfully. 'Already you've made more progress than Miss Botham, the speech therapist, and she's been going there over a year.'

Rachel frowned. 'I can't understand why she's so terrified of going there. Speech therapists aren't usually fearsome creatures.'

'I can't understand it, either. Although to be fair, she's always all right once we get there. It seems as if it's just the thought of going that upsets her.' He got up and went to the door. 'It's not as though it's helping her to speak, though.' He sighed. 'I have to take her again next Thursday; I think I'll make this the last visit. It only wastes everybody's time. But one likes to feel one's making some effort. . . . ' He looked over his shoulder at Rachel. 'Would you like to come too? Maybe you can shed some light on why she acts so strangely.'

Rachel followed him to the door, screwing her eyes against the light, 'Yes, I'd like to come. But I think you're probably wise to stop the visits as she finds them so upsetting.'

She reached his side as she spoke and they walked back to the house together. Richard opened the door and stood aside for her to go in. 'I think the visits to Miss Botham are superfluous, anyway, now that we've got you,' he remarked, closing the door.

Rachel turned, surprised at his last phrase 'now that we've got you', but he was not there and she saw him outside, passing the window on his way to the garage to get his car and go into Ardenbeg.

It was then that she remembered the previous evening's parting and realised that facing Richard hadn't been difficult after all, contrary to what she had feared. She also realised that she was not cured of her infatuation for him.

Pleased with her success, Rachel attacked Melanie's education with renewed vigour. Progress was slow, but gradually she began to draw a little, odd tortured drawings that Rachel couldn't understand at all. On good days, too, she would copy words and figures and even do simple sums. But on bad days she would spend the entire morning running to the window, looking for Ben, restless at being cooped up indoors. On those days Rachel would take her out if the weather was not too bad and let her ramble in the woods and over the

Estate. Her favourite spot was the waterfall and she would stand watching the water cascading from boulder to boulder in rapt fascination until Rachel called her away. They often seemed to meet Ben on these rambles, and studying him Rachel wondered if Aunt Rose could possibly be right. Could Celia Duncan have been going to meet Ben on the night she was killed? He was certainly a very attractive and personable young man. But—a vision of Richard Duncan rose before her—surely no woman in her right senses would contemplate leaving Richard for Ben.

She was considering this as she walked home with Ben one afternoon. Melanie was behind them, chasing the rabbits who were so tame that they almost allowed her to catch them and seemed to enjoy the game as much as she did.

'Did Celia often walk in the woods with Melanie?' Rachel asked.

'Now and then. Not often,' Ben replied.

'What was Celia really like, Ben? You've told me she was beautiful, Alistair says she was "bonny"—that was his word, too. But I can't discover much about her as a *person*. I don't think my aunt cared for her much,' she added as an afterthought.

Ben smiled. 'No, Celia didn't exactly make a hit with Rose. But then you'd hardly expect her to, would you? Rose was not likely to welcome any girl who wanted to take her precious Richard away from her, was she? Old nannies can be more possessive than mothers, you know.'

'Mm. I hadn't thought of that.'

'As to what Celia was like, have you never seen a photograph of her?'

'No, never.'

He fished in the pocket of his jeans and brought out

a tattered wallet. From it he drew a snapshot of a flaxen-haired girl, sitting on a gate, in a figure-hugging white sweater with a scarlet spotted scarf knotted at the neck, her long legs encased in scarlet trousers. Her head was thrown back and she was laughing. She looked radiant.

'I took that,' Ben said proudly. He replaced it in his wallet lovingly. 'Beautiful, wasn't she? Why such a lovely girl had to die. . . .' He shook his head. 'It was wicked.'

'My aunt says. . . .' Rachel hesitated, half afraid to go on.

Ben took her arm and smiled down at her as they emerged from the trees and approached the house. 'Take my advice and don't pay too much attention to what Rose says, Rachel, my dear. Oh, I know she's your aunt and perhaps I shouldn't say it to you, but when Richard married Celia Rose had to take a back seat. She even had to leave the big house and move to the cottage. After twenty something years do you think she would take kindly to that? Do you imagine she *liked* being deposed? She's only human, when all's said and done. She resented Celia, she was jealous of her. You could hardly expect her to welcome her with open arms. I'll bet you've not found anyone else who's disliked Richard's wife.'

Rachel shook her head. 'No, that's true, I haven't.'

'There you are, then.' Ben smiled down at her and squeezed her arm affectionately. Rachel smiled back at him. He was really rather like a big brother, she thought happily.

Richard was at the corner of the house. Plainly he had watched them come from the woods and was waiting for them.

'Where's Melanie?' he said curtly to Rachel.

'Chasing rabbits, I believe,' Rachel said with a smile.

'You're supposed to *know* where my daughter is and what she's doing,' he snapped. He turned to Ben. 'And my father pays you to work on the Estate, not to take leisurely rambles with every pretty girl in sight.' He turned to go. 'Three o'clock tomorrow afternoon,' he threw over his shoulder to Rachel. 'That's when Melanie has to be at the speech therapist's. I'll pick you both up here at two. Don't be late.' He marched off into the house.

Ben grinned. 'Don't mind him. I expect he's had a bad day at the fishing,' he said.

But Rachel hardly heard. Richard had called her a pretty girl.

Thursday was one of Melanie's restless days. Rachel suspected it was because of the impending visit to Dunglevin, but she made no comment. Instead, she took the little girl for a walk up to the waterfall after barely an hour's schooling. Ben did not make an appearance, which seemed to disappoint Melanie slightly, but even so she seemed calmer when they returned to the house.

After lunch, at which Richard did not appear, Rachel sent Melanie to her room to put on her prettiest dress while she, Rachel, changed into a smart cream suit trimmed with coffee and cream check to match the blouse she wore with it. She even tied her hair back with the same colour ribbon, then stepped back to survey her appearance. Scraping her hair back made her look far too stern, she decided, pulling off the ribbon and shaking her hair free. That was better. She picked up her handbag and went to find Melanie.

Richard had just come in with the car when they arrived at the garage.

'I'm not late, am I? I was having lunch with Moira,'

he said, giving his hair a quick comb with a glance in the driving mirror. 'It's her birthday today. No, don't get in there,' as Rachel began to open the back door of the car, 'there's room for both of you in front here.' He leaned over and opened the passenger door for her. Melanie hung back. 'Oh, heavens, child, you're not going to be tiresome, are you?' he snapped impatiently.

Rachel took her hand and got in beside her. It was obvious that Richard was not in the best of tempers.

'I had wondered about taking Melanie somewhere for tea after she's seen Miss Botham,' she said hesitantly. 'But if you're in a hurry to get back I could bring the Mini, then we wouldn't hold you up.'

Richard had his hand on the ignition as she spoke. For a moment his eyes rested on his little daughter, then he looked at Rachel. 'That's a very good idea,' he said slowly. Rachel gathered up her things and made to get out of the car. 'No, sit still.' He started up the engine. Suddenly he smiled at her and Rachel's heart did a little skip, much to her consternation. 'We'll all go. We'll go to the Patisserie, it's years since I've been there. Would you like that, Melanie?'

Melanie nodded, a queer, jerky little nod. Rachel could see that she was too tensed up over going to speech therapy to feel much enthusiasm for anything else. She clung tightly to the older girl's hand all the way from Glencarrick and through Ardenbeg and as the road rose above the loch Rachel felt the tension increasing even more.

Richard glanced at his watch. 'We've no time now, but we'll come back this way and stop at the vantage point. I've got binoculars with me today so you'll be able to see right across the Kyles to the mainland.'

'Kyles?' Rachel repeated.

'Narrows. Straits. Strip of water between the islands.

Have you never heard that expression before?'

'No.' Rachel, her arm still comfortingly round Melanie, craned her neck to see what she could of her surroundings; but Melanie had her head buried and refused to look. However, as Rachel talked to her and soothed her gradually she began to relax and although she was clearly far from happy most of the tension had gone by the time they reached Dunglevin.

Miss Botham was a large woman smothered in jangly jewellery. It was plain from her manner that she considered Melanie a waste of her time. But she went through the motions while Rachel watched and Melanie patiently and unco-operatively waited for the lesson to be over.

'Not an easy child to deal with,' Miss Botham said over Melanie's head to Rachel. 'I think, myself, that obstinacy plays a large part in her problem.' She sighed. 'But I'm inclined to agree with Mr Duncan that bringing her here to me is a sheer waste of everybody's time.'

Rachel put her arm round Melanie. She was not going to discuss the problem in front of the child herself. 'Thank you for trying, Miss Botham,' was all she said.

She led the little girl from the room. Miss Botham was right, of course, Melanie had taken the whole thing with what could only be described as utter boredom. But, and this surprised Rachel, she had shown no fear or tension in the speech therapist's presence. In fact, there was no hint of the terror she had shown at the outset of the journey. It was as if she had simply resigned herself to the inevitable. Yet, and this puzzled Rachel more than anything, what was there about Miss Botham to frighten a child, anyway? She was a perfectly ordinary—if a trifle bizarre—woman, doing a somewhat difficult job. Without, in Melanie's case, any success whatsoever.

Richard, waiting outside, raised his eyebrows questioningly as they emerged. Rachel shook her head to indicate that she would discuss it with him later and he took the hint.

'Right,' he said. 'Are you ready for tea, then?' He smiled at them both, obviously making a great effort to reach his daughter.

'Yes, I'm starving,' Rachel said, supporting him. 'How about you, Melanie?'

Melanie patted her tummy and licked her lips. 'You,' Rachel laughed, ruffling her hair, 'you're always hungry!'

Richard drove to the Patisserie and parked the car. 'Do you think I'm smart enough to take two young ladies out to tea?' he asked Melanie, brushing an imaginary speck of dust from his suit and adjusting his tie. Melanie looked up at him and nodded shyly. Father and daughter found it very difficult to communicate in any way, Rachel realised sadly.

They ate toasted teacakes, scones and sticky buns, finishing with an enormous ice cream gateau which made Melanie's eyes light up with delight.

'You'll be sick and I'll ruin my figure,' Rachel laughed, giving Melanie a second helping and accepting one for herself.

'I used to come here for a special birthday treat when I was a lad,' said Richard, licking his fingers. 'These things taste just as good now as they did then.' He was enjoying himself, Rachel could see, and he was more at ease with his little daughter than she had ever seen him. Melanie, for her part, was sparkling with excitement, her cheeks flushed and her brown eyes dancing. Perhaps, Rachel thought, this was the moment to break through Melanie's barrier of silence.

'Melanie,' she said gently, 'I think you should say thank you to your father for bringing us out to tea, don't you?'

Melanie looked from Rachel to Richard and back again, her eyes suddenly filled with sadness. She opened her mouth and licked her lips, then she slid off her chair, went to Richard and putting her arms round his neck she planted a kiss on his cheek. Then as if embarrassed by what she had done, she went and buried her head in Rachel's lap.

Richard fingered his cheek thoughtfully. 'I don't ever remember her doing that before,' he said thoughtfully.

The journey home was uneventful until they reached the vantage point high above the loch. Melanie had been half asleep on Rachel's shoulder, but when the car stopped she woke, obviously frightened.

'Were you dreaming, dear? It's all right, we've only stopped to admire the view,' Rachel reassured her as Richard rummaged for his binoculars.

'We'll be able to see better from over there,' he said, opening the door and unfolding his long legs.

Rachel opened her door to get out too, when suddenly Melanie sat bolt upright in her seat, clutched Rachel's hand and let out a piercing scream, her face a mask of absolute terror. For fully half a minute she screamed, her whole body rigid, then, just as suddenly, she crumpled into Rachel's arms and lay there, sobbing.

Rachel comforted her as best she could, mystified by such an outburst. 'I think we'd better take her right home,' she said to Richard. 'Have you ever known this to happen before?'

He shook his head, obviously shaken. 'That's the first time she's uttered a sound since ... for two years,' he finished, as mystified as Rachel had been. He turned the car and drove down to Ardenbeg and home to

Glencarrick with one eye on the road and one eye on his daughter, now exhausted in Rachel's arms, her face white and tear-streaked.

'I'll get her bathed and straight up to bed,' Rachel said when they arrived at Kilfinan House.

'Yes, I think that's probably the best thing.' Richard brushed his hand gently over Melanie's head. 'I wish....' he began, then changed his mind. 'I'll put the car in the garage,' he finished.

Rachel had bathed Melanie and was just tucking her into bed when there was a tap on the bedroom door and Richard came in.

'Is she all right?' he whispered.

Rachel nodded and tiptoed to the door with a backward glance at Melanie who, with her faithful teddy clutched in her arms, was already almost asleep through sheer exhaustion.

Richard stood outside in the corridor with Rachel, his face perplexed. 'I can't understand it,' he whispered.

'Come into my room, we can talk there,' Rachel invited. 'I'll leave her bedroom door ajar so that I'll hear if she wakes.' She opened the door opposite to Melanie's bedroom and Richard followed her into her sitting room and flung himself down into an armchair.

Rachel knelt down and switched on the electric fire with a slight shiver.

'Cold?' he asked.

She shrugged. 'A little.'

He looked at her and his eyes were suddenly filled with compassion. 'I'm sorry, Rachel,' he said, 'I really had no right to saddle you with my worries. Melanie.... Oh, I don't know.' He leaned forward and put his head in his hands and Rachel had an almost irresistible desire to put her arms round him and comfort him. Suddenly he looked up, his face tortured. 'What am I going to *do* with her? What's *wrong* with the child?'

Rachel sat back on her heels. 'At least,' she said slowly, 'we've discovered today that her fear of going into Dunglevin has nothing to do with being afraid of Miss Botham. The vantage point on the road above the loch is what terrified her today. It seems to me that she's afraid to even drive past that spot. Have you any idea why?'

She looked at Richard.

'No, none at all,' he said. 'But of course, you're right. Why has it never occurred to me, though? I've been taking her to speech therapy all this time assuming that is was simply the thought of going that frightened her—you see, she was always perfectly all right by the time we reached Dunglevin, and mostly I'd take her home the other way, coming in at the head of the glen so we didn't use the scenic road at all on the way home. It never occurred to me....'

'It probably would never have occurred to me either if you hadn't stopped the car there and she hadn't been so petrified,' Rachel pointed out fairly. 'I don't imagine you'd ever stopped there with her before.'

'No, you're right, I hadn't.' Richard stared down at his hands.

'Is there anything special about that place?' Rachel asked. She hesitated. 'I mean, is that the spot where ... Celia ... your wife's car ...?'

'No,' he interrupted, 'but it was along that road.'

'Oh.' Rachel could see that it was still painful for him to talk about his wife's death. He leaned back in the chair and closed his eyes, a frown creasing his brow. Suddenly he opened them. 'It couldn't have been anything to do with that, though. Melanie wasn't with Celia when the accident happened. It was late at night and Celia was alone.'

'I see.' Rachel got up off her knees and took off her jacket, hanging it over the back of a chair. Then she stood leaning on the chair back. 'But *something* must have happened to Melanie at some time at that spot. Something, the memory of which still fills her with terror. What on earth could it be?'

Richard shook his head. 'I've no idea at all.' He looked up and his eyes met hers and held them. Suddenly the familiar surge of emotion filled her, almost choking her with its intensity, and she gripped the back of the chair to steady herself.

In a moment he was by her side. 'Rachel, are you all right? Is something the matter?' He put an arm round her shoulders solicitously and tilted up her face. 'You've gone quite pale.'

She resisted the urge to rest her head on his shoulder and twisted away from him, not trusting herself to speak until she had put the width of the table between them. 'I'm fine,' she said shakily. 'A little tired, that's all, and dying for a cup of coffee. Would you like some, too?'

'I would, indeed.' He was regarding her strangely. 'I'll go and make it, if you like.'

'No, no, I'll go. It won't take a minute,' she managed a breathless smile. 'Perhaps you'd like to put a record on while I go and do it. You've put quite a varied selection at my disposal. You're fond of music?' She knew she was prattling but she couldn't help herself.

'Very.' He was still looking at her oddly.

'Good. So am I.' She reached the door. 'It'll be interesting to see if our tastes coincide.' She escaped and hurried along the corridor and down the stairs. Her cheeks, which had been cold, were now flaming and she pressed her hands to them. What was the matter with her, behaving like a lovesick schoolgirl over this man? The kitchen was cool and she tried to compose herself as she made coffee and prepared cheese and biscuits—anything to keep her hands and her mind busy. One thing was certain; Richard Duncan must never know the devastating effect he had on her. That would be just too humiliating.

With this in mind she carried the tray back upstairs. It had begun to blow outside and the wind gusted flurries of rain on to the window, making the atmosphere in her comfortable sitting room seem even more cosy and inviting. By the time she got back Richard had discarded his jacket and had rolled up his shirt sleeves, revealing tanned muscular forearms, and was busy selecting a record from the rack. 'I hope you like Brahms,' he said, without turning round.

'I do. Particularly his first symphony.' She put down the tray as the strains of music began. 'Oh, that's exactly what you're playing!'

'It's one of my favourites, too.' He got to his feet and took the coffee she had poured for him and went over to the nearest armchair. Rachel poured a cup for herself and went and sat opposite to him. The scene was altogether too domesticated and intimate for her peace of mind. She sipped her coffee and gazed at the flickering effect the electric fire gave out. Synthetic flames. Unreal. Illusory. Exactly like the situation she was in at this moment. She closed her eyes and gave herself up to fantasy and the music.

'Majestic, isn't it?' said Richard, as the last notes died away. He came over to her and took her empty coffee cup and refilled it for her. 'What would you like now? A contrast? Mozart, maybe? Mendelssohn?'

'The Mendelssohn violin concerto, please.' She allowed herself a brief glance up at him as she spoke.

He put her coffee on a stool and sat down on the

arm of her chair, his face full of concern. 'Rachel, what's wrong with you? You're as jumpy as a kitten. Are you worried about your aunt?'

'Yes,' Rachel clutched at the straw he offered, 'I am. Your father says she'll be all right, he's spoken to ... to....' her mind was whirling at his closeness and she couldn't think straight.

'Archie Murdoch,' he finished for her. 'Yes. And if Archie says she'll be all right you can take his word for it she will be.' He spoke gently, which only served to increase the turmoil within her. She escaped by getting up and going over to the record player, but before she could select another record he had come up behind her.

'I think perhaps I should go,' he said. 'It's quite late and you are obviously not yourself. No doubt this business with Melanie has contributed to that, as well as your concern over Rose.' He sighed. 'I'm sorry, Rachel. Instead of coming here to recover from your own misfortune you seem to have become caught up in problems here which we'd no right to burden you with. But please try not to worry.' He turned her to face him. 'Look, I've told Moira I'll take her sailing next week, I've not got a particularly busy week with fishing, so it seemed a good opportunity. I thought we'd go for a whole day and sail to one of the islands. Why don't you come, too? And Melanie, of course.' He smiled slightly. 'I'm sure it won't hurt her to have a day off "school".' He emphasised the last word slightly. 'Anyway, it can always be called an educational trip, can't it?'

Clinging to the last threads of her self-control, Rachel managed to smile back. 'I'm sure Melanie would enjoy that.'

'And you?'

'Oh, yes. Me, too.'

'Good. I'll let you know which day nearer the time. It depends to a large extent on the weather, of course.' He studied her for a few seconds more. 'I've never known you to look quite so strained,' he remarked.

'I expect I'm tired,' she whispered, wishing he would go, yet wanting him to stay.

'Mm. Yes, I suppose that's what it is.'

She had never known him to be so concerned and solicitous. This was a new Richard and one she found it almost impossible to resist.

He nodded to himself, satisfied with her explanation. 'Well, goodnight, sleep well, and thank you for your concern over my little girl.' He tilted up her face and bent his head to drop a light kiss on her forehead, but suddenly his arms came round her in a vice-like grip and his mouth found hers in a kiss that seemed to her to last light years and sent her soaring through un-dreamed-of galaxies of stars.

At last he almost threw her from him. 'I'm sorry, I shouldn't have done that. It was unforgivable of me,' he muttered, turning away. 'It was just ... a man has needs ... it won't happen again, I promise you.' He picked up his jacket and hurried from the room, leaving her, the back of her hand pressed to her bruised lips, with tears running down her cheeks. Whether the tears were of humiliation, hatred or happiness or a mixture of all three Rachel had no idea, but by the next morning, in the cold light of day, she realised that of the three happiness had very little part in it.

CHAPTER SEVEN

IT was not many days before Rachel regretted accepting Richard's invitation to a day's sailing. Apart from the fact that she realised that the less time she spent in his company the better it was for her peace of mind, there was Moira.

Moira had taken to calling at Kilfinan House on the flimsiest of pretexts and she called just after lunch one afternoon as Rachel was preparing to drive with Melanie into Ardenbeg. Melanie had run off to find Ben and Rachel was beside the Mini calling her when Moira's car swept up the drive. As always, Moira was immaculately turned out, in honey-gold slacks that looked as if she had been poured into them and a brown, equally close-fitting jumper. She wore a silk screen-printed scarf in oranges, browns and yellows, at her neck, caught high on the shoulder with a large expensive-looking cameo brooch. Her auburn hair was secured with an ornate tortoiseshell comb.

Rachel went forward to greet her, feeling very ordinary in her gingham summer dress and sandals, a cardigan slung over her shoulders for when the day became chilly.

'Where's Rick?' Moira was probably less than half an inch taller than Rachel, yet she managed to give the impression of looking down at her.

'He'll be out all day today. He went early this morning and he left a message that he wouldn't be in until late tonight.'

'Oh!' Moira seemed to take this as a personal affront.

'He's supposed to be taking me sailing this week, but he hasn't said which day.'

'I believe we're going the day after tomorrow, if the weather's right,' Rachel told her.

'We? Are you coming, then?' Again Moira managed to look down at Rachel, and this time there was no mistaking the disdain in her expression.

'Richard thought it might be good for Melanie,' Rachel explained wretchedly.

'And of course you'll have to come too, to look after the child,' Moira's face cleared a little. 'I hope she's not prone to seasickness.'

'I hope so, too. I want her to enjoy herself.' Rachel managed to smile at Moira. 'I'm sure Richard will be in touch with you about the final arrangements. Of course, you do realise that he can't make definite plans until the last minute, don't you?' She was trying hard not to feel antagonistic towards the other girl, but finding it very difficult.

'Naturally,' Moira said coolly. 'He told me that when I saw him last night.'

Melanie came running from between two trees, but as soon as she saw Moira she stopped, hovered for a moment like a bird, and then sped off towards the barn.

'That child's becoming like a wild animal,' Moira announced. 'I can't understand Alistair wanting to keep her at home. Richard is right. She should be at school; that's one thing over which he and I are in complete agreement, and that's where she'll go as soon as we're....' she stopped and smiled graciously at Rachel. 'Of course, I'm not denigrating what you're doing, Rachel, don't think that; in fact, I'm sure it's working very well. As a temporary measure, of course.'

'Miaow!' thought Rachel. She looked at the other

girl's long scarlet fingernails and saw that they were indeed like claws. Moira McLeod, she realised, would make not only a dangerous enemy but also an uncomfortable friend.

Moira got back into her car. 'I'll ring Rick tonight,' she said, swinging it round and driving off at breakneck speed in a cloud of dust.

Miraculously, Melanie appeared and hopped into the Mini beside Rachel, showing a gap-toothed grin.

'My goodness, you've lost a tooth!' Rachel pretended to be surprised although the tooth had been hanging on by a thread for nearly a week. 'What have you done with it?'

Melanie held out her hand proudly and showed Rachel the tiny little tooth in her palm.

'Put it under your pillow tonight. You never know what the fairies might leave in its place. Now, shall we go and watch the boats at Ardenbeg?'

Melanie nodded happily.

But on the way to Ardenbeg Rachel had another idea.

'I'm going to take you along the high road to Dunglevin, Melanie,' she told the little girl quietly. 'I'm going to take you to the place you don't like, that for some reason frightens you so much, and I'm going to show you that you've nothing to fear. I shall be with you all the time and if you can you must show me what it is that you are so afraid of. Then I'll be able to help you.' She glanced briefly at the child. 'Do you understand, dear? There's nothing to be afraid of, I only want to help you.'

Melanie didn't move, but Rachel could sense the sudden tension in the little body beside her. She drove through Ardenbeg talking all the time, occasionally giving Melanie's hand a quick squeeze. As the road rose so Melanie crept closer to her and her face began to pale.

'Now, it's all right, we're not going to stay here long,' said Melanie as she parked the car at the vantage point high above Eilean Dorcha. Melanie had cowered back into a corner of her seat and covered up her eyes. Gently, Rachel drew her towards her and put her arms round her. 'You're quite safe, Melanie. I'm with you. I won't leave you.'

At these words Melanie flung her arms round Rachel's neck and began to cry.

'There, there, it's all right, darling. You're quite safe with me.' Rachel opened the car door. 'Come along, let's get out and have a look at the beautiful scenery.' She swung her legs out of the car, but Melanie clung to her and would neither leave the car herself nor allow Rachel to. 'But why not, Melanie? What are you afraid of?' Rachel asked. But Melanie couldn't tell her. She clung to Rachel, sobbing, and there was nothing Rachel could do but hold her close and talk to her comfortingly. At last she became calmer, and still holding her firmly Rachel managed to ease her out of the car and over to the railings.

'Look, there's the little lighthouse where we went for a picnic with Ben. Do you remember?' Rachel pointed to the spit of land beside the island far below where the tiny derelict lighthouse stood.

At first Melanie hung back, but then her curiosity overcame her and she peered down through the trees and undergrowth growing on the mountainside to the scene below, still clinging tenaciously to Rachel.

'One day we'll walk down to the lighthouse from here,' Rachel told her. 'There's a pathway, can you see it, over there? It winds down through the trees, see?'

Melanie's eyes widened and she stared, fascinated.

'Want to go and have a look?' Rachel smiled encouragingly, but Melanie shook her head vehemently and pointed to the car.

'All right, if you've had enough. We'll come back another time. You won't mind so much now, will you?'

Melanie shook her head again, but more uncertainly this time. The tension, although it was still there, had lessened, but her grip on Rachel's hand had not.

They drove back to Ardenbeg and watched the boats on the loch for a little while and then they went home. Rachel was thoughtful. She had still not discovered what it was about that spot that had terrified Melanie, but maybe in time. . . .

Wednesday was the day of the planned sail to Arran, and it dawned with a light mist over the glen which heralded a hot day. Melanie was beside herself with excitement and kept getting in the way as Rachel packed the picnic.

Bring plenty of warm clothing, Richard had warned, it's never as warm on water as it is on land. There's always a cool breeze.

Rachel and Melanie were both wearing old jeans and T-shirts and Rachel packed two thick sweaters apiece and rolled up raincoats in case it rained, which didn't seem likely.

Moira arrived looking like a model from the Boat Show. All her clothes, even down to her brand-new deck plimsolls, were absolutely right for the occasion and had plainly been purchased specially. Her auburn hair was pulled back in a ponytail fastened high on her head and her make-up was discreet. As always, she made Rachel feel ordinary and insignificant—plain, was perhaps the best word.

They were going in Richard's nineteen-foot sailing

cruiser *Thursday's Child*—named after Melanie, he had once told Rachel, with a bitter twist to his mouth, 'although that child should have been born on a Wednesday,' he'd added, 'Wednesday's child being full of woe!' There was no mistaking his disappointment in the child he had fathered.

He was waiting for them at Ardenbeg pier when they drove up in Moira's car. *Thursday's Child*, the boat he kept simply for his own pleasure, to sail when he had not arranged fishing parties in *Celia*, a much bigger and heavier boat, was ready and waiting at anchor and he rowed the two girls and Melanie out to it with long, easy pulls on the oars. Then, after helping them aboard and boarding himself, he made the dinghy fast behind and they set sail.

'If you'd like to take the tiller, Moira,' he directed, 'and keep a straight course, Rachel can help me with the sails. Melanie, you sit there, in that corner, and keep out of the way.'

Rachel found the next five minutes the most confusing of her life. The cockpit seemed full of ropes, which were not called ropes at all but halliards and sheets. But she managed to follow Richard's instructions without making too many mistakes.

The day was perfect. With just sufficient wind to fill the sails the sun was warm on Rachel's face. It was like a day out of time, she thought as she sat with Melanie on the foredeck, watching the bow rise and dip with the slight swell of the sea. Richard had relieved Moira at the tiller and she was sitting with him in the stern of the boat with an expression on her face like a cat that's stolen the cream. This was going to be her day and nobody was going to spoil it for her.

Rachel gave a mental shrug. Richard had invited her today as Melanie's governess, to bring Melanie on an 'educational trip'. Nothing more. Moira had made it abundantly clear that Richard belonged—or soon would—to her; his behaviour in her, Rachel's, sitting room a week ago was best forgotten. If that was possible. Her only consolation was that she was in no danger of betraying her own feelings if it should happen again because it never would. Richard had been quite definite about that.

They sailed through the Kyles and out into the Sound. Here the water was so deep it was like sailing on a sea of black ink. Rachel had never seen water so dark yet so calm and unmenacing. She felt strangely at peace. Melanie was enjoying every minute and her eyes were everywhere, but mostly she was fascinated by the great sea-birds that wheeled high above the water before plunging, their wings folded back, like arrows, straight down into the sea, only to come up again with a fish, which they would swallow whole.

'Look at those birds! It's a marvel they don't knock themselves out, they must hit the water at a terrific speed,' Rachel called over her shoulder to Richard.

'They're gannets,' he called back. 'Their skulls are specially protected against this. I believe the bone is honeycombed or something—just another one of Mother Nature's provisions for her children. Keep your eyes peeled for whales, too. You can sometimes see them in these waters.'

But Melanie was not interested in looking for whales just then, she was hungry. So Rachel took her into the cabin to prepare lunch; hot soup and rolls, fruit and coffee, which they all ate out in the cockpit.

Moira was very quiet and ate little, confining herself to an apple and a cup of black coffee.

'Aren't you feeling well, Moira?' Richard asked.

Moira put on an heroic smile. 'Yes, I'm fine. Really.

A bit of a headache, that's all. Please don't fuss.'

Rachel looked at her. She didn't look at all well. 'Perhaps if you went and sat on the foredeck the motion of the boat would be slightly different and you would feel better,' she suggested.

'I'm *not* feeling seasick, if that's what you're thinking,' Moira said sharply. 'I merely have a headache. And I'm perfectly all right where I am, thank you.' She tucked her hand through Richard's arm.

'Look!' Richard freed his arm to point to the coast of Arran. 'There's the Sleeping Warrior.'

'Sleeping Warrior? Whatever do you mean?' Moira sounded a little petulant.

'Can't you see? The contours of the land form the shape of a man; see? he looks as if he's lying between those two mountains. That's why he's called the Sleeping Warrior.'

'Yes, I can see him,' said Rachel. 'Look, Melanie, can you see his big tummy with a row of buttons down his coat? And his head—there, look, with his big nose?'

Melanie nodded, her imagination working overtime.

'I don't see. . . .' Moira pushed her sunglasses up into her hair and leaned against Richard to get a better view, squinting against the sun as she did so. 'Oh, yes, I think I can see his hat.' She lowered her sunglasses but remained clinging to Richard.

Rachel collected together the lunch things and went below to wash them and stow them away. When she came back she found Richard teaching Melanie how to helm, much to her surprise and Melanie's obvious delight. Moira was sitting beside them, trailing her hand over the side and looking thoroughly bored.

Arran loomed larger and larger, its steep cliffs barren and forbidding, and Rachel began to wonder why Richard had chosen such an uninspired place to sail to. It came as a complete surprise to her when they rounded a bleak-looking point and quite suddenly found themselves sailing into a beautiful sheltered bay, where the water was deep and so clear that you could see the bottom, and the mountains rose on three sides, green and littered with sheep. A little town, hardly more than a row of houses, edged the shore and on a grassy spit jutting out from the shore into the bay stood a ruined castle.

Rachel rubbed her eyes. 'It's just like a fairy tale!'

'But it isn't. It isn't a mirage, either, it's quite real. Unexpected, though, isn't it?' Richard smiled.

'It's perfect,' Rachel breathed.

'Do you think there'll be a chemist's where I can buy aspirin?' Moira asked.

'Sure to be. No doubt people get headaches even in a place like this,' Richard told her cheerfully. 'We'll moor here and I'll row you ashore.'

He moored *Thursday's Child* and rowed them all ashore in the dinghy. Immediately, Moira went off to buy aspirin and Rachel found a shop where she could buy Melanie icecream. 'I'll take her up the hillside a little way,' Rachel told Richard. 'It will do her good to run around. She's been very good, but she's had to sit relatively still on the boat for quite a long time.'

'That's a good idea, we'll all....' Richard began.

'Rick, there's a teashop over there. I need a drink to help me swallow these aspirins.' Moira caught his hand. 'We'll see you later,' she called to Rachel.

Richard said nothing but went with Moira, politely putting his hand under her elbow to guide her across the road.

Rachel felt saddened as she followed Melanie up the mountain track, the little girl scampering happily ahead. Moira was going to marry Richard, there was no doubt about that. Rachel recalled David McLeod's words at the Midsummer Ball, 'My sister is a very determined woman. She knows what she wants and she usually gets it.' And Moira McLeod wanted Richard Duncan, that anyone could see with half an eye. All except Richard, it would seem. It would appear that he was the last person to realise this. He invariably treated Moira in a polite and friendly manner, apparently not even noticing her possessive gestures. Rachel sighed. Was he still grieving so much over his dead wife that he couldn't see how Moira was trying to manipulate him? How he must have loved Celia! With a start of guilt Rachel thought of Keith, her dead fiancé, and realised that he had not been in her thoughts much at all lately, and when she did think of him it was with affection but no longer with any sense of loss.

She sauntered on up the hillside, leaving the track and wandering between rocks and boulders bedded in mossy grass, singing to herself as she went. After a while she sat down on a rock and looked down into the bay. It was a picture-postcard view with the sea and sky a perfect blue against the green hillsides and little white houses. She could pick out *Thursday's Child* from the other boats scattered in the bay by its cream hull and tan sails. How excited Richard must have been at the birth of his little daughter, and how proud of her he had once been to name his boat after her. Yet now she was little more to him than an embarrassment. She looked round for Melanie to point the boat out to her.

'She's up there, by that rock, watching rabbits,' Richard said from beside her.

'Oh!' Rachel turned in surprise. She had neither seen nor heard his approach, so deep in her own thoughts had she been. 'But where's Moira?'

'Drinking tea in the teashop.'

'Didn't she want you to stay with her?'

'I suggested that it would be better for her to rest quietly alone, without the effort of conversation.' There was the merest hint of a smile on his face as he spoke, so faint that Rachel was not sure she hadn't imagined it. He sat down and rested his elbows on his knees. 'This is a perfect place,' he said softly. 'Quite perfect. I'm glad you came.' He turned round to look for Melanie as he spoke, so Rachel was not quite sure she heard those last words aright.

Suddenly he put his hand out and gripped hers. 'Listen,' he whispered, and inclined his head to where Melanie was playing, hopping from stone to stone, rock to rock, oblivious of everything and everyone, absorbed in a world of her own. 'She's *humming*!'

Rachel strained her ears. There was no mistaking it, Melanie was humming the same song Rachel had been singing as she walked up the hillside. 'Don't let her know we can hear,' she murmured, turning away. 'She may be self-conscious and stop.'

'But it's happening, something's happening!' Richard was still holding her hand; she had never seen him so animated. He caught her other hand and pulled her to her feet, his eyes alight with pleasure. 'And it's all due to you, Rachel. You're really getting through to her.' He stood looking down at her and there was no mistaking the warmth in his eyes. 'She's very fond of you, you know,' he said softly.

She licked her lips, fighting the emotions that his nearness always aroused in her. 'I'm very fond of her,' she whispered.

He stood looking down at her for a moment more and then Melanie came running down towards them, her arms outstretched to embrace them both, knocking them even closer together as she ran full tilt into them.

'And how many rabbits did you see?' Rachel managed to ask, her voice a trifle breathless. Richard was still holding both her hands. 'Six?'

If she had hoped for another miracle she was disappointed. Melanie shook her head and mutely held up four fingers. But she was grinning happily.

They went down the hillside together, with Melanie in the middle, holding hands and singing, Richard's deep voice blending well with Rachel's. But although Melanie was almost bursting with good spirits she didn't join in. It didn't matter. Rachel and Richard had heard her once; they knew she could if she wanted to; the chink in her armour of silence was widening.

Moira was sitting on a seat overlooking the bay. 'You've been an awfully long time,' she said petulantly.

'Have we?' Richard said in surprise. 'Well, you could have come to meet us.' He looked at his watch. 'We mustn't be too late starting back because I would like to get home before it gets too dark. I think we've got time to take a look at the castle before we go, though.'

They explored the castle and bought sandwiches and scones at the little teashop before beginning their journey home. Moira seemed in better spirits now that her headache had gone and remarked with a sigh as they rowed back to *Thursday's Child*, 'What a perfect spot for a honeymoon!'

Rachel made no answer to this and Richard appeared not to have heard.

The journey back was something Rachel felt she would never forget. The tranquillity of the evening, the sounds of the boat swishing gently through the water and the wind in the sails gave her a sense of being at peace not only with herself but with the world as a whole. Time seemed to be standing still. With

Melanie asleep on her lap—the little girl had finally succumbed to the exhaustion of her exciting day—she sat in the stern of the boat, Richard at the tiller opposite her with Moira beside him, her head on his shoulder, once again looking a little green although she insisted that she didn't feel ill.

'How long before we arrive home?' she asked once, lifting her head briefly from its resting place. 'There's a programme on television I want to see. I'm sure you'd be interested in it, too, Rick.'

'It'll be at least another hour,' Richard replied. 'The wind, although it's in our favour, is not very strong so we're not making headway all that fast. I could of course start the motor, but. . . .'

'Why don't you do that?' Moira said eagerly, and at the same time Rachel put in involuntarily, 'Oh, no, that would spoil everything.'

'It might wake the child,' Richard decided, putting an end to any argument.

Moira made an impatient gesture, obviously bored by the inactivity, and even the sight of seals basking on Lamont Point in the sunset could not fire her with any enthusiasm. It had not been Moira's kind of day at all, but for Rachel it was a day that would always have a special place in her memory.

It was dusk by the time they arrived back at Arden-beg. Melanie had woken, but she was still sleepy.

'Moira, you'll drop Rachel and Melanie off at Kilfinan House, won't you? I've things to clear up here,' said Richard as he put them ashore.

'Yes, of course. Then shall I come back for you?'

'No. I've got my car here, thank you all the same.'

'We could go for a drink. . . .'

'Some other time. In any case, I thought there was a programme on television you wanted to watch.'

Moira sighed heavily. 'I expect it will be over by the time I get home.'

Richard smiled. 'Not if you hurry, my dear. Look, Rachel and the child are ready and waiting; they won't hold you up.'

Moira picked up her bag and turned away—flounced off, would have been an apt description had it not been impossible to flounce in skin-tight denim dungarees rolled up to the calf and deck plimsolls.

Rachel suppressed a smile and followed her to the car, dragging a weary Melanie behind her. The two girls hardly spoke on the way back to Glencarrick, Moira was silent with pent-up frustration and Rachel simply didn't want to talk and break the spell the day had woven over her.

Back at Kilfinan House she bathed Melanie and put her to bed, where the little girl's head hardly touched the pillow before she was asleep; then after relaxing in a warm perfumed bath herself she dressed in a long flowered skirt with a cream top, for no other reason than it made her feel feminine and seemed a fitting way to end the day—even though she was spending the rest of the evening alone.

She had just settled down with a book when there was a tap at the door. Richard stood there. He, too, had showered and changed and was wearing grey trousers and a blue shirt that was open at the neck.

'I wondered if you'd like to come out for a drink with me,' he asked, his tone almost diffident. 'There's not much night-life around these parts, I'm sure you must get bored, but we could go into Ardenbeg.'

Rachel felt herself flushing. 'I'd love to, but Melanie.... I can't leave her. After all, I am her ...' she somehow couldn't bring herself to say the word governess, '... she is my responsibility.'

He rubbed his chin. 'Yes, I was forgetting. I've been so used to leaving her in Rose's care. And it's no use relying on my father. He's very fond of Melanie, but he never knows how to handle her. In any case, he's gone to Dunglevin to visit Rose tonight.'

'He goes most nights, doesn't he?' said Rachel.

Richard smiled and nodded. 'They've always been very good friends. I think he must miss her a great deal, although he would never admit it.' He hesitated. 'Well, it's ridiculous standing and talking at your door like this. As you say you can't come out for a drink, and obviously you can't, come to my study and we'll have one there. That way, we'll still be able to keep an ear open for the little one. All right?'

Rachel nodded. She knew she should say no, that she was only storing up heartache for herself, but she couldn't refuse.

Together they looked in at Melanie. No longer did she sleep screwed up with tension; now her whole body was more relaxed and her lips were parted in a faint smile.

'She even begins to *look* more like a normal child,' Richard whispered as they left the room.

He led the way to his study and poured a drink for her and one for himself. 'This seemed to me a suitable way to end a very nice day,' he said, his eyes meeting hers as he raised his glass. 'Oh, damn!' The phone rang on the desk and he moved to answer it.

Rachel was almost relieved. It gave her a chance to compose herself again. Why, she asked herself, did she allow this man always to have this shattering effect on her? Even now, as she sipped her drink, her hands were shaking.

'Yes, all right, Moira, I'll come straight away.... Of course.... Yes, I'll be with you in ten minutes.... No,

of course I don't mind.' He slammed down the receiver
and picked up his glass, draining it in one gulp.

'That was Moira, as you probably gathered. She's
in a tizzy because all her lights have failed and she's
there alone. She wants me to go and have a look at
them for her. I expect it's the generator, it's always
playing up.' He was shrugging into his jacket as he
spoke. 'It shouldn't take long to put right.'

Rachel got up from her chair and went to the door.
'It must be rather frightening for her, alone in that
isolated farmhouse in the dark,' she commented

'Oh, she's got plenty of candles. This isn't the first
time it's happened,' he said casually. Then, with more
concern in his voice, 'I'm sorry to drive you away like
this, Rachel. Oh,' he handed her her glass with an
apologetic smile, 'do take your drink with you.'

He left and Rachel went back to her own room. She
made her drink last a very long time, sipping it while
she thought about Richard and Moira. Moira intended
to marry him, of that there was no shadow of doubt.
But Richard? On the one hand he seemed quite oblivious of her charms and intentions, while on the other
she had only to snap her fingers and he went running
to her. He could hardly leave her in the dark with no
electricity, a little voice from the corner pointed out
reasonably.

But she had been in bed a very long time before she
heard his car returning home up the drive. Could a
generator that was always playing up and wouldn't
take long to put right suddenly have become *that* much
trouble?

CHAPTER EIGHT

RACHEL didn't see Richard for several days and she began to wonder if he was avoiding her, although she could think of no possible reason why he should. She continued with Melanie's schooling, making silent and very slow progress with her. But it was progress all the same, and she was convinced that behind the shutters that the little girl had apparently put up to keep the world out there was a very active and intelligent brain.

The afternoons were still devoted to the open air. Melanie loved her rambles in the woods and up to the waterfall, and often they would go further afield in search of Ben, working in some far corner of the Estate. Rachel was very fond of Ben in a sisterly kind of way. He was good-natured and fun to be with. But he would never, ever, be anything more to her than a very good friend, she was sure of that. And for his part there had had only ever been one woman in his life, it was becoming increasingly plain each time Rachel talked to him, and that woman was Celia Duncan, whom he had worshipped from afar, it would seem; putting her on a pedestal high above all other women.

Celia Duncan. What an extra special person she must have been to arouse such passions in the people around her! Undying devotion in Ben; Richard, who, having been married to her, could never bring himself to even look at another woman; and on the other hand Rose, who, although she had difficulty in displaying any form of emotion, could not conceal her dislike—almost hatred—of Richard's wife. Not for the first time Rachel wished she could have met this beautiful enigma.

On one of her frequent visits to her aunt Rachel managed to steer the conversation round to Celia.

Rose, after two months in hospital, was now allowed up to sit in a chair on the terrace. It was getting near to the end of the summer, although the sun was still quite warm, and she was dressed in a forget-me-not blue housecoat in soft wool. A rug was draped over her knees. Since she had been in hospital her thick iron-grey hair had been cut and styled and showed signs of gently waving; her face, too, had filled out. Each time she saw her aunt it struck Rachel more forcibly how attractive the older woman was becoming.

'In another month I may be allowed home—to convalesce, they say,' Rose told her in her pleasant low voice. It had a hint of a chuckle in it. 'I don't know about convalescing, though, there are so many things I want to do. Is my cottage all right?' Her voice became anxious. 'It's not damp. is it? We've had quite a lot of rain since I've been in here.'

'Your cottage is perfectly all right, Auntie,' Rachel laughed. 'Ben and I take it in turns to light a fire there. I can assure you it's not damp.'

Rose pursed her lips disapprovingly at the mention of Ben's name. 'Is Melanie with Ben this afternoon?' she asked.

'No. She's gone to play with Mrs Munroe's little granddaughter. Jeannie sometimes comes in with Mrs Munroe so Melanie knows her and they play quite well together in a funny sort of way.'

'That's good. I don't like her spending so much time with that man.' Rose pulled the rug up round her and Rachel noticed that even her hands looked younger now that they were no longer work-roughened.

'She spends very little time with Ben nowadays,'

Rachel said, 'but I can't understand why you should object to her being in his company, anyway. He's kind and gentle and I'm sure he's very fond of her.'

'Hmph!' Rose pursed her lips tightly again and looked out over the bay.

Rachel sighed deeply. 'I wish you'd tell me what it is you have against Ben, Auntie. I know you don't like him, but you never say why. I think he's rather nice, myself.'

Rose looked at her sharply. 'That wolf's not turned his charm on you, my girl, has he?'

Rachel laughed aloud. 'Oh, Auntie, whatever do you mean? Ben's no wolf!'

'That's what *you* think.' Rose turned and looked her niece full in the face. 'All right, I'll tell you, my girl.' She took a deep breath. 'The night Richard's wife was killed—do you know where she was going?'

Rachel shook her head. 'I only know it happened on the high road above the loch. The Dunglevin Road.'

Rose nodded. 'That's right. And do you know *why* she was going to Dunglevin? Alone? At midnight?'

Again Rachel shook her head.

'Use some common sense, my girl. There *could* only be one reason for a fly-by-night like Celia Duncan—she was going to another man, of course. And the other man was Ben Carson. It's my guess she wasn't coming back, either.' Rose lay back in her chair and closed her eyes.

Rachel digested this for several minutes. 'Have you any proof?' she asked at last.

'Only what my eyes and common sense tell me.'

'What about Richard?'

'Richard? Do you imagine his pride would allow him to admit that his wife had gone off with another man? The whole incident was handled very discreetly, naturally. The story put out was that Celia had had an urgent call to her sick mother.' Rose shrugged. 'It wasn't true, of course. Celia had no mother. At least, if she had she wasn't on good terms with her, because she wasn't at her wedding, I do remember that.' She paused to let Rachel think this over before she added, 'In any case, as she never reached Dunglevin there was nothing to prove or disprove. But I'd seen the way she'd carried on with that Ben Carson, and anyone could see with half an eye that he was besotted by her.' She leaned forward as far as her restricted movements would allow. 'And *that* week-end he was away—the only time he's ever been away, because he never goes home.'

'Where is his home?'

'Some remote Hebridean island, I believe. He never even talks about it. But that week-end he'd gone home for his father's funeral.' Rose shook her head. 'Coincidences like that simply don't happen.'

'Did anyone else suspect? Alistair? Moira?'

'Alistair, bless him, never sees further than the end of his nose. He imagines that all marriages are like his own was, idyllically happy. Till death us do part. It would never occur to him that Celia could have preferred another man to Richard, his son.'

'What about Moira?'

Rose made a face. 'If Moira suspected anything she wouldn't say. After all, Fate had played right into her hands, hadn't it? With Celia out of the way the field was clear for her.'

Rachel was silent for a while. 'Do you think Richard and Moira will marry?' she asked at last.

'Eventually, yes. But not until Richard's business is on a more sound footing. Richard would never be content to live on his wife's wealth.'

'But Kilfinan. . . .'

'Kilfinan won't come to Richard until his father

dies, which, please God, won't be for a very long time.'
Rose yawned, 'I'm sleepy now, my girl. I think it must
be all the pills they keep giving me. Pills for this and
pills for that—sometimes I can't think straight, I feel
so dopey.' She regarded Rachel thoughtfully. 'I've
talked an awful lot, too, this afternoon, about things
best forgotten.' Her eyelids drooped. 'But you'll see
now why I worry about the child ... with *him*. He's
only kind to her because she's Celia's daughter....'

Rachel got up and kissed her aunt. 'I'm sure you've
no cause to worry, Auntie', she said gently.

She left Rose and made her way to the car park, too
full of her own thoughts to stay and shop in Dunglevin
as she sometimes did. She drove home as far as the
vantage point above Eilean Dorcha and here she stopped and left the car. A walk was what she needed to
clear her muddled thoughts. She climbed the stile and
began to follow the footpath Ben had pointed out to
her the first time they had come to this spot. It was
rough going as it wound down the mountainside between trees and bushes and she was relieved when she
came to a clearing with a strategically placed seat overlooking the island. It was aptly named Eilean Dorcha,
Rachel mused; with its dense, almost black vegetation
it did indeed look a dark island, and she wondered
briefly if there was some sinister history attached to it
or whether it was just that it looked so dark against the
brilliant blue of the loch.

She sat down on the seat and let her thoughts wander
back to her conversation with Rose. She frowned.
Apart from complaining about the pills they made
her take Rose seemed entirely rational. Yet her story
was far-fetched, to say the least. Mentally, Rachel
ticked off each item. One. Celia had been killed driving
along the Dunglevin road; not at the vantage point

where the Mini was now parked, but at a point not far distant from it. That much was undisputed fact. Two. Rose insisted that Celia was going to another man, and that that man was Ben Carson. This was Rose's idea, no one else had even hinted that this might be so, in fact, if anything quite the reverse. Alistair had obviously liked his sons's wife; Ben had idolised her from afar, and Richard—Richard still had eyes for no other woman. On the other hand, Rose, on her own admission, had disliked Celia, and had, according to Ben, been jealous of her. Understandably, perhaps. As Ben had pointed out, nannies could be very possessive and to be relegated to the cottage after over twenty years must have been hard to take. Then there was Ben. Of course, *he* wouldn't want anyone to believe Celia was going to another man, particularly if he was the man. And if he had not been the man surely his faith in her would have been shattered, which it clearly was not. Rachel sighed. It all seemed such a tangle, with Melanie, poor disturbed little Melanie, right in the middle of it all. Suddenly she caught her breath. Maybe that was why Ben, who of all people might have been able to break Melanie's barrier of silence, had made no effort to encourage the little girl to talk. Maybe if she talked she would tell too much....

Slowly, she retraced her steps back to the Mini, so lost in thought that she didn't notice how steep the climb was. She paused and looked out over the Kyles towards the mainland before getting back into the car. What had happened to Celia Duncan was all in the past. It was, as Rose had once said, useless to rake it all up. Yet it still seemed to hang, like a cloud, particularly over Melanie, and until it was brought out into the open would she ever be cured?

*

Several weeks had gone by since the trip to Arran, and although Rachel had given her every encouragement Melanie had not allowed the chink in her armour to widen beyond humming to herself when she thought nobody was near. Rachel was baffled. Melanie seemed happy and relaxed now, yet something was still holding her back from communicating like a normal child.

'It's disappointing,' Rachel confessed to Richard. 'I thought she was really beginning to open up when she began humming, but....'

'Hasn't she done it again since the day at Arran?' Richard searched her face anxiously.

Rachel didn't meet his gaze. They had met at the door as she and Melanie were off on their afternoon walk and she was very conscious of the fact that her slacks had seen better days and that her sweater was old and baggy. He, for his part, had just come from a meeting and was extremely smart in a dark grey suit, beautifully cut, with a blue shirt and a darker blue tie. As always the sight of him made her senses misbehave and she caught her breath. Was this man always going to have this devastating effect on her?

She answered his question with her eyes firmly fixed on the mountain rising behind Kilfinan House. 'She hums to herself when she thinks nobody can hear,' she told him. 'I've tried to encourage her by singing with her, at which she immediately stops. I've tried to make her talk by deliberately turning my back on her when she make signs to me, but that doesn't work, either. She'll go to endless lengths to make me understand. But she won't speak.'

'I see.' He tapped his briefcase thoughtfully with one finger. 'And where are you going now?'

'For our walk. We always go in the afternoon if the weather isn't too bad. The fresh air does her good and she particularly likes it up by the waterfall.'

'Have you seen the big one, up on Ben Binnean?' He nodded towards the mountain towering over the landscape.

'No. You warned me once about the stupidity of wandering about on mountains, so Melanie and I stick to the parts we know, mostly the Estate, unless we go somewhere in the car and then walk.' Rachel looked round for Melanie, who had run off somewhere.

Richard looked at his watch. 'Give me five minutes to change and I'll take you up Ben Binnean. It's true it wouldn't be wise for you to try it on your own, but I've scrambled over it since I was knee-high to a grasshopper and I know it like the back of my hand.' He turned to go into the house. 'Oh,' he added, over his shoulder, 'shoes, not sandals. Both of you. The going can be quite rough.' He disappeared inside and Rachel went to find Melanie, who was watching rabbits just inside the woods.

Five minutes later, in stout walking shoes, they set off with Richard, who had exchanged his city suit for old corduroy trousers and a sweater that was even more shapeless than Rachel's.

'This way.' He led them up a grassy path that had once been a cart track and over a five-barred gate. The track wound upwards, gradually narrowing into nothing, and the heathery slopes became steeper and craggier as they climbed. They could hear the rush of the waterfall long before they reached it, but then suddenly there it was, roaring angrily from a great height to spill and tumble into a deep ravine where it was lost in a mist of froth and spray.

'They call it Eas Mhor—Great Waterfall. Impressive, isn't it?' said Richard.

Rachel held Melanie's hand tightly, sensing the awe

in the little figure. Even she had to suppress a shudder at the sheer ruthless power that nature had unleashed. 'It's ... I've never seen anything like it,' she said, at a loss for words. 'It looks—cruel. And disappearing down into that huge hole ... it looks as if it might easily go right down into the middle of the earth.'

'Actually, it divides up and part of it comes out lower down as Eas Beag, Little Waterfall, the one you so enjoy visiting.'

'At least it's more friendly by the time it becomes Eas Beag,' Rachel remarked. Don't you think so, Melanie?'

Melanie nodded; her eyes were wide with wonder at the majestic sight and she kept very close to Rachel's side.

'Look,' Richard had climbed a little higher, 'you can just see the house down there between the trees. Looks small from here, doesn't it?'

'Almost like a doll's house. I didn't realise we'd climbed so far up.' Rachel bent to Melanie. 'See, Melanie, that's Kilfinan House, where we live. Doesn't it look tiny?'

Melanie nodded again. Suddenly she let go Rachel's hand and darted across to a boulder a little distance away.

'Melanie!' Richard called sharply. 'Don't run off. The mist can roll in almost without warning, you must stay with us.'

But Melanie appeared not to hear. She was intent on something she had seen in the heather and went running off.

'Melanie!' Rachel ran after her and caught her. The little girl tugged at Rachel's hand. 'What is it, dear, what can you see?' Rachel bent down to see what had caught the little girl's attention. 'Oh, it's a frog. That's because the ground here is damp. Frogs like soggy ground and pools. He's quite attractive, isn't he?'

Suddenly the frog gave an enormous leap and was gone.

Rachel stood up and looked round for Richard. He was nowhere to be seen, but rolling towards them was a thick white wall of mist, swallowing everything in its path. This was what he had warned them against. In seconds it had enveloped them, isolating them in a dense, eerie blanket with no sound but the roar of Eas Mhor, which was no comfort at all, nearby.

Rachel shivered and put her arm round Melanie, whose face was a mask of sheer terror. It had all happened so quickly that she'd had no time to check where she was and now all sense of direction had gone; she didn't know whether Richard was to her right or left, in front or behind. And somewhere, very near, was a deep ravine into which the great waterfall was cascading.

'It's all right, darling. We'll just stay here, completely still, until it clears.' She tried to sound confident and reassuring, but she could hear the tremor in her voice as she comforted Melanie. 'It'll go as quickly as it came, I daresay.'

Melanie huddled against her, petrified. Then, suddenly, she took a deep breath and lifted her head. '*Daddy!*' she screamed.

Almost immediately Richard's shadowy form appeared and Melanie flung herself at him. 'Daddy!' she sobbed again. 'Daddy!'

'It's all right, little one, I'm here,' Richard soothed, holding her to him and stroking her hair. 'There's no

need to worry. We're quite safe. I've got a compass, I
know the way back, it's perfectly all right.' All the time
he was speaking his eyes were on Rachel and the expression in them was a mixture of pride, relief and
elation. 'She spoke!' his eyes said. 'Melanie spoke!'

And Rachel, her eyes bright with tears, rejoiced
silently with him.

Together the three of them made their way carefully
down from the grey, cottonwool world of the mountain
mist. Richard had no difficulty in directing and as they
reached the lower slopes the mist became wispy and
thin, finally disappearing altogether.

When they arrived back at Kilfinan House Rachel
sent Melanie to wash while she prepared tea.

'Will you have some with us?' she asked Richard,
who had perched himself on the corner of the dresser.
'I'm sure Melanie would like that.'

'Why not?' Richard smiled one of his rare smiles.
'The mist on the mountain has resulted in a real break-
through. We've cause to celebrate, haven't we?'

Rachel paused in the act of buttering bread. 'I
think we still have to go carefully,' she said thoughtfully. 'Melanie isn't suddenly going to become gar-
rulous. But now we know she *can* speak, so we must
simply be patient and encourage her. If we push
her too hard she could easily slip right back into her
shell.'

Richard rubbed his chin. 'Yes, you're probably right.
I notice she hasn't said anything else.'

'I think she's very delicately balanced at the moment.
A wrong move and we could be right back to square
one.' Rachel drew the knife slowly across the butter.

He came over to where she stood and looked down at
her. A lock of dark hair had fallen across his forehead,
making him look boyish. 'I think perhaps my father

was right after all,' he said, leaning over and helping himself to a thickly buttered crust. 'It was his idea that Melanie should have a governess, and you're certainly very good with her, Rachel. You've made more progress with her in two months than anyone else has in two years.' He munched the crust, his eyes resting on her thoughtfully. 'I really am most grateful to you.'

Rachel wasn't sure whether she dropped the bread knife or threw it down. She only knew she wanted to shout at him, 'I don't want your gratitude. I want more than that. I'm only human, can't you see I'm in love with you?' But she didn't say any of those things. She bent down to pick up the knife but he reached it before her and as he handed it to her his hand brushed hers.

'Thank you,' she said. What else was there to say?

Melanie didn't speak through tea, though Richard tried to encourage her to talk in spite of Rachel's warning glances. He was obviously disappointed at her lack of co-operation.

But as Rachel tucked the little girl up in bed and kissed her goodnight Melanie reached up and put her arms round Rachel's neck. 'Goodnight, Rachel,' she said, slowly and deliberately.

'Goodnight, darling. Would you like to say goodnight to Daddy, too?' Rachel could hardly trust herself to speak.

Melanie nodded.

'All right, I'll go and fetch him.'

She went along to Richard's study and knocked at the door. He had changed, she noticed as he opened it; he was wearing beige flared trousers and a dark brown rollneck shirt. Behind him, in the pale green jump suit that suited her so well, Moira was comfortably draped in an armchair, a drink in her hand. It was a cosy and intimate scene.

'Melanie would like to say goodnight to you,' she told Richard briefly.

His face lit up. 'I'll come right away.'

'Don't be long, Rick. The dinner starts at eight and there are drinks first.' Moira's voice was proprietorial.

'We've plenty of time.' He came out and closed the door behind him, following Rachel up the corridor to Melanie's bedroom.

Rachel watched as he stood looking down at his little daughter, his expression a mixture of perplexity and affection. He leaned over her and stroked the side of her face gently with one finger. 'Goodnight, little one,' he said softly.

'Goodnight, Daddy.' The words came slowly, as if she had to think carefully before uttering them. Her velvety brown eyes, as she gazed up at her father, were dark and unfathomable.

'Goodnight, little one,' he repeated, straightening up. Rachel noted with surprise that he hadn't kissed her.

They left Melanie and Rachel closed the door quietly. In the corridor Richard hesitated as if there was something he wanted to say.

Rachel looked at her watch. 'Moira is waiting. You'll be late for your dinner,' she said flatly.

'Yes. It's a Young Farmers thing. Moira asked me if I'd go along with her.' He shrugged. 'I usually escort her on these occasions.' Still he hesitated.

'I hope you have a nice evening.' She went to her own door, but he got there first and opened it for her.

'Thank you.'

He looked down at her; they were standing very close, too close for Rachel's peace of mind. 'Thank *you* for everything.' He bent his head and Rachel had the feeling that he was about to kiss her, but the door further up the corridor opened and Moira's voice said, 'Aren't you nearly ready, Rick?' at which he straightened up and turned away.

'Yes, I'm coming, Moira.' Rachel was almost sure there was a note of exasperation in his voice, but later she realised that she must have imagined this because it was very, very late when she heard his car return after his evening out with Moira McLeod. Sometimes Rachel felt she had come to Scotland only to find more heartache than she had left behind in Suffolk.

As Rachel had told her aunt, she and Ben were keeping an eye on the cottage, lighting fires as and when they felt it necessary. Rose's fears that her home might be damp were entirely unfounded, the cottage was built like a castle, with walls a foot thick in places and the stout oak doors and heavily latticed windows were guaranteed proof against the worst weather.

One afternoon, when Melanie was playing happily with Mrs Munroe's granddaughter, Jeannie, in the barn, Rachel went to the cottage to find some books Rose had asked Alistair for the previous evening.

Ben was already there. He had lit the fire and was fixing some shelves up over the sink.

'Rose has hinted that she'd like shelves up here several times, so I thought I'd do them while she's out of the way,' he said, measuring and marking the wall and then tucking the pencil behind his ear.

'You and Rose don't exactly hit it off, do you?' commented Rachel with a faint smile.

'Oh, it's not that. But she wouldn't appreciate shavings and wood chips all over her kitchen, so it's best to get it done and the mess cleared away before she comes home.' He screwed a bracket on the wall and stood back to eye it up. 'All the same, you're right, we don't get on. At least, Rose apparently dislikes me. Personally, I've nothing against her, except she's a bit starchy, but I suppose she can't help that.' He screwed the other bracket on to the wall and laid the shelf on it. 'There, that's about it. Do you think there's room for another one above it, Rachel?'

Rachel studied the wall for a moment. 'No, I think I'd put a narrow one underneath. It'll be easier for her to reach, she's not very tall.'

'Good idea.' He measured the wall again.

She watched in silence for a while, then she said, 'Did Richard's wife ... I mean, was she unfaithful to Richard, Ben?'

'Blast!' Ben dropped the pencil he was holding in the sink, retrieved it and marked the wall. 'No, of course not. What makes you think she was?'

Rachel frowned. Was his reply a shade too vehement? She thought of the photograph he had shown her of Richard's wife, a radiant, almost coquettish photograph. A photograph Ben himself had taken. 'Something Aunt Rose said. She told me that Celia was on her way to meet another man when she was killed.'

Carefully, almost too carefully, Ben finished screwing brackets on the wall and placed the shelf in position. Then he gathered up his tools and put them in the bag. When he had done this he sat down in the armchair on the opposite side of the fire to Rachel. His face was white and set.

'Your aunt seems to have overlooked one vital thing in her slanderous accusations,' he said, 'and that is that Celia's car went over the cliff on the way *back* from Dunglevin.'

Rachel bit her lip. 'Are you sure?'

'As sure as anyone could be in such a situation. The place where the car went over would be exactly right for anyone taking the bend too wide and fast on the way *from* Dunglevin. If she'd been going the other way the car would have gone over at a completely different place. It couldn't have gone over where it did, there were crash barriers, bushes—oh, the angle would have been all wrong. I've been there, paced it out; it's quite obvious what happened.'

'But why should she have been coming back? If she wasn't going to another man but to visit her mother who was ill....'

Ben made a gesture with his hands. 'I'm only telling you what I know. Celia was killed coming *back* from Dunglevin. I'm not concerned with what everybody else says; all I know is that it should never have happened to such a beautiful woman, so full of life....' He got up from his chair and began searching for a brush and dustpan to sweep up the shavings he'd made in an effort to recover his composure.

Rachel watched him in silence, more confused than ever. He had loved Celia, there was no doubt about that. But had she been going to him on the night of her death? Or was she, as he claimed, killed on her way back from Dunglevin? In which case why had she gone there in the first place? Then again, was Ben simply saying these things to put everyone off the scent? She sighed. Instead of discovering answers all she'd succeeded in doing was uncovering more questions.

She got up from her chair. 'I'd better go and look for the books Aunt Rose has asked for,' she said, changing the subject. 'She told Alistair they were in the bookcase in her bedroom.'

'I'll just finish clearing up here, then I'll be on my way,' said Ben.

Rachel went upstairs to find the books. Rose's bedroom was as neat as the rest of the house, with a pretty chintzy bedcover to match the curtains. The highly-polished floorboards were dotted around with scatter rugs and Rachel decided she would have to have a word with her aunt about such highly dangerous floor covering. Carpets would be not only safer but warmer.

She selected the three books Rose had asked for and turned to go, but the rug slipped, taking her feet from under her, and she went down heavily, with a cry and a thud.

'Rachel, are you all right?' Ben's voice came from the foot of the stairs.

'I—I think so. The rug slipped. . . .' Before she could get to her feet Ben was beside her. 'No, nothing seems to be broken.' Gingerly, she felt her elbows and knees. 'It was a stupid thing to do, I'd only just been thinking that I must persuade Auntie to carpet this room because these rugs were dangerous.' She laughed ruefully.

'Are you sure you're all right?' Ben asked again, anxiously.

'Perfectly, thank you.' She smiled at him reassuringly and together they left the bedroom.

'Oh! I do beg your pardon.' Richard was standing at the foot of the stairs and from his expression there was no mistaking his interpretation of Rachel and Ben leaving the bedroom together, particularly as Ben had his arm round Rachel, innocent though it may have been. 'The back door was open so I came in to investigate.' His tone was icy. He turned away. 'I would suggest that if you're going to make a habit of this kind of thing,' he laid heavy emphasis on the last words, 'you make sure that the doors are closed in future.' He left then, without giving either of them a chance to explain.

Ben grinned, his spirits restored. 'And I hadn't even kissed you! However, that's soon put right.' He put his hand under her chin and his mouth came down on hers.

Quickly, Rachel twisted away. 'No Ben. I don't feel that way about you, any more than you do about me. You're my very good friend, that's all.'

He sighed. 'You're right, Rachel. I'm fond of you, too, but not in that way.' He shook his head. 'Sometimes when I look at you I think I must be out of my tiny mind.'

Rachel preceded him down the stairs. It was quite true. Ben would never be any more to her than a very good friend, while Richard.... Richard. After this afternoon's events, mistaken though he had been in his conclusions, how would she ever face Richard again?

CHAPTER NINE

As it happened, facing Richard again was not as difficult as Rachel had anticipated. He came to the playroom where Rachel was giving Melanie her daily
lessons one morning about three days after the incident
at Rose's cottage.

'Hullo, Daddy,' said Melanie, beaming, in the slow,
precise way she had. Her speech was still limited and
spasmodic, but Rachel was optimistic. One thing she
had found, though, it was useless to try and force the
little girl to talk; she would only speak when she
chose to. It was clear that Melanie would never be a
chatterbox.

'Hullo, little one.' Richard went over to her and
ruffled her hair. He seemed a little more at ease with
her these days. 'And what are you learning today?'

Melanie pointed to her Ladybird reading book.

'Are you going to read to me, then?'

Melanie shook her head.

'Why not?' He shot a questioning glance at Rachel,
who managed to convey to him not to press her. 'All
right, I'll read it to you.' He began to read, 'Peter and
Jane like apples. Here is a plum tree....'

'Apple tree,' Melanie corrected seriously, automatically pointing to the word he had misread.

'Oh, yes, so it is.' He read on, with Melanie correct-
ing all his deliberate mistakes, for several pages. Rachel
was gratified to see that her little pupil didn't miss a
trick and that Richard was both surprised and pleased
at his little daughter's progress.

He got up to go. 'Moira's brother, David, will be home next week,' he told Rachel, his voice and expression impersonal, 'and I've invited them over for a meal on Thursday evening. They usually come over when David is home. Do you think you could sort out menus and things with Mrs Munroe? I don't know what she's like when it comes to slightly more sophisticated cookery; her everyday menus are nothing to write home about, I must say. We miss Rose in that direction.'

'I'll have a word with her,' Rachel promised. 'I'm sure we can work something out between us. Will Alistair be there? I'll need to know numbers.'

'No, it'll just be the four of us.'

Rachel raised her eyebrows. 'Four?'

'You'll partner David.' He looked directly at her for the first time. 'That is, unless you have a prior engagement.' There was no mistaking his meaning.

To her fury, she felt herself blush. 'I've no prior engagement,' she said quietly.

Melanie was restive after her father had gone and refused to co-operate at all. In fact, in a fit of temper she swept all her books from the table and jumped on them. Rachel sighed. This was a new pattern of behaviour and she wasn't sure whether it indicated progress or regression. In any case the whole process was a case of two steps forward and one back. She made Melanie help her to pick up the books and then took her for a walk.

Mrs Munroe tightened her lips at the prospect of a dinner party and it was only Rachel's promise to organise everything that pacified her. So it was that Rachel spent most of the day of the dinner party in the kitchen preparing the food herself, while Mrs Munroe stood by lamenting on the unnecessary expenditure and fuss and insisting that plain wholesome food was more digestible. Rachel didn't argue. The food Mrs Munroe served was certainly plain and probably wholesome, but not always particularly digestible!

David and Moira arrived promptly at seven; the meal was timed for quarter to eight. Rachel had left Mrs Munroe careful instructions and a strict timetable to work to, so everything was under control by the time she went upstairs to bath and change. Melanie was to join them until her bedtime at seven-thirty.

Rachel chose to wear a dress she had bought in Dunglevin on one of her visits to Rose. It was a mix 'n match print of delicate greens and browns on a cream background, with shoe-string shoulder straps and a closely fitting bodice which moulded her figure and showed off her tiny waist, falling in tiers of gathers to the ground. It was simple and very feminine. She brushed her hair until it shone and let it fall loose to her shoulders.

'Nice,' said Melanie, when she went to see if the little girl was ready. Melanie, too, had a long dress. Hers was in white seersucker with tiny yellow flowers. It had a deep flounce at the hem and a wide yellow velvet ribbon at its high waist. Rachel had also fastened a yellow ribbon in Melanie's hair.

'You look nice, too, Melanie,' Rachel smiled, and took her hand, noticing that it was unusually clammy. Melanie looked pale, too. Rachel hoped she wasn't going to be ill.

They went downstairs and greeted Richard, who was pouring drinks for Moira and David. He poured lemonade for Melanie.

'Thank you,' Rachel prompted, but Melanie mutely nodded her thanks in the old way and declined to speak.

David McLeod was as handsome as she had remembered, his chestnut hair perhaps a little longer and more straggly but still thick and wavy. He was obviously pleased that Rachel was to be his partner for the evening and impatient for Melanie to be sent to bed so that he could have her all to himself.

Melanie, for her part, clung to Rachel in a jealous and possessive way which was almost embarrassing. And she refused to speak at all, much to Richard's annoyance. Even Rachel was glad when it was time for Melanie to go to bed.

'What on earth's got into her?' Richard hissed as they passed his chair.

Rachel shook her head. Who could know what went on in the strange little girl's mind?

Melanie clung very tightly to Rachel when she kissed her goodnight. In fact, it was only by letting her have Droopy to cuddle that Rachel could leave her and return downstairs. Droopy was the long-eared, lugubrious-looking fluffy dog that sat on Rachel's bed and held her nightdress.

Dinner was a success and for that Rachel was grateful. They had stuffed mushrooms, cutlets of venison (from the deer culled from the Estate) in chestnut purée followed by oranges in Grand Marnier. Everything was delicious, Mrs Munroe had followed Rachel's timetable rigidly, but it wasn't until she plodded in with the cheeseboard that Rachel felt she could begin to relax.

David had no such inhibitions. The wine Richard had chosen had loosened his tongue and he paid Rachel the most extravagant compliments and overtly tried to hold her hand across the table. Desperately, she tried to make him keep his distance, conscious that Richard, although deep in conversation with Moira, was nevertheless watching everything that was going on.

Coffee and liqueurs were served in the lounge, where a huge fire burned in the grate against the chill of the early autumn evening. Two deep settees stood adjacent to the fireplace and Moira settled herself in one of these, patting the space beside her. 'Come on, Rick. Come and be cosy,' she invited.

Richard smiled briefly and sat down, whereupon she curled her feet under her and nestled up to him, her head on his shoulder.

Rachel had no choice but to sit on the settee opposite, where David soon joined her, his arm carelessly across the back. He ran a strand of her hair through his fingers. 'Just like spun silk,' he murmured, his hand finding the nape of her neck.

She leaned forward and began to pour coffee, set out on the low table between the settees, her hand shaking a little as she did so. She had never felt more miserable and uncomfortable in her life.

'Leave mine on the table,' said Moira, as Rachel handed her a cup. She clearly didn't want to change her position, close to Richard.

'Thank you.' Richard managed somehow to lean forward far enough to take his cup without dislodging Moira and his eyes met Rachel's as he did so. Rachel couldn't read the expression in them; they were dark, almost black, and they seemed to bore right down into her soul as he held her gaze—was it accusingly, or disdainfully? Whatever it was it sent a surge of colour to her cheeks and made her drop the sugar spoon. Why did this man have such an effect on her? Why could he not leave her as completely unmoved as David McLeod, who she was sure would need little encouragement to begin a fullscale affair with her, or Ben, who would never be anything more than a very dear friend?

With trembling hands she poured David's coffee and handed it to him, nearly tipping it straight into his lap as an agonised scream came from Melanie, upstairs.

Rachel got up, kicked off her flimsy gold sandals and rushed for the stairs. It wasn't until she reached Melanie, who was screaming and sobbing alternately, that she realised Richard was right behind her.

'It's all right, darling, I'm here.' Rachel gathered the little form into her arms. 'It's all right. Calm down.' She had never seen Melanie so distressed since the day at the vantage point. Melanie clung to her tightly. 'Don't go,' she cried in a strangled voice, 'don't leave me!'

'I won't leave you, Melanie, never fear.' Rachel cradled her in her arms and rocked to and fro.

Richard standing helplessly by, a worried frown on his face, handed Rachel a large white handkerchief. 'Her tears are making your dress wet,' he explained.

Rachel smiled her thanks and wiped Melanie's face. She was calmer now, her tears had gradually subsided and although her eyes were wide with fear, she managed a small smile.

'Was it a bad dream, little one?' Richard asked kindly.

Melanie nodded.

'Would you like to tell us about it, then you can forget it ever happened? Things are never so bad if you talk about them.' He sat down on the bed close to Rachel and leaned over to smooth the hair away from his little daughter's face.

Melanie looked at him for a moment, then shook her head and buried it on Rachel's breast. Richard continued stroking her hair, his other hand resting on the bed behind Rachel to support his weight. Rachel could feel the rough texture of his jacket on her shoulder; he was so close to her that she could feel the beat of his heart, and she realised that she and Melanie together were almost encircled in his arms. She held her breath.

Suddenly, Melanie lifted her head and smiled at them both. 'Better now,' she said. 'Nasty's gone.'

'Good.' Rachel lowered her back on to her pillow.

'Stay with me.' Melanie clutched Rachel's hand.

'All right, darling, just for a while.' She was glad; she had no wish to return downstairs to David's unwelcome attentions, nor to watch Moira's possessive manner with Richard.

'You'll come down when she's asleep?' Richard bent his head to whisper in her ear as he left.

'Of course.'

He stood looking down at his little daughter for several moments, then he bent and dropped a light kiss on her forehead. 'Goodnight, little one,' he said softly.

Rachel stayed with Melanie much longer than she intended. Sitting quietly beside the little girl she began to realise how busy her day had been preparing for Richard's dinner party, and then the added strain of being polite to David and Moira, neither of whom, it suddenly struck her, she cared for in the least, had all taken their toll. She was very tired. She was asleep almost as soon as Melanie.

When she woke it was quite late. Hurriedly she went to the top of the stairs, just in time to hear David say, 'I'll bring the car round. You wait inside, Moira,' as he went out of the front door.

She slipped quietly down the stairs. Halfway down she was able to see through the open door into the lounge, She stopped. There, standing by the fire, locked in a passionate embrace, were Richard and Moira. As she watched, rooted to the spot, Richard lifted his head and saw her. For a moment his gaze held hers, then, deliberately he bent his head and kissed Moira again.

Rachel turned and went back to her room, where she undressed and got into bed as quickly as she could and lay gazing into the darkness, dry-eyed and miserable. Why, oh, why couldn't she hate Richard Duncan?

Melanie's birthday was on the twenty-first. Rachel had made and iced a cake for her, but she still insisted that she didn't want a party—indeed, other than Mrs Munroe's Jeannie who was there to invite? So Rachel suggested a visit to the cinema in Dunglevin where a Walt Disney film was showing.

'Oh, yes!' Melanie clapped her hands. 'And Daddy must come. Then we'll have tea at the Pat ... Pat. ...'

'Patisserie.' Rachel helped her out. Her speech was becoming more fluent now, but she still had complete days when she said little or nothing and Rachel felt they still hadn't got to the bottom of Melanie's problem. 'Very well, but *you* must ask him.'

Rachel was not too happy with Melanie's idea. She had avoided Richard as far as possible since the night of the dinner party and the prospect of a birthday tea at the Patisserie with him filled her with misgivings.

Misgivings he, apparently, did not share. 'Oh, dear, I have a fishing trip booked for that day, little one,' he said. 'I'll see if I can alter it, but if I can't, let's see, the film should be over by a quarter to five—I could meet you for tea. How would that be?' He smiled at Melanie, ignoring Rachel, standing nearby.

'I'd like that,' said Melanie.

'All right, I'll see what I can do.' He made a note in his diary, ruffled Melanie's hair affectionately and went off, without even acknowledging Rachel's presence. He's rude, Rachel told herself fiercely. Rude and ill-mannered and I hate him. But she knew she didn't.

The day of Melanie's birthday was overcast, but it didn't dampen her spirits in the least. Excitedly, she opened her cards and presents; an expensive ball game that looked as if it was more suitable for a boy from Alistair; a dainty dress which Rose had sewn and embroidered herself and which Melanie insisted on wearing immediately; Rachel had bought her a large selection of felt pens in their own leather case and even Mrs Munroe's Jeannie had sent a tiny, rather oddly-shaped pottery bowl that she had made herself at school. Richard had left a card and a message, 'I'll give you your present at tea. Love, Daddy.' There was not so much as a card from Moira.

'No school today,' Rachel announced.

'Because I'm seven.'

'That's right, because you're seven. What shall we do?'

'Go to the waterfall.'

'All right. The little one, Eas Beag. We can't go up the mountain to Eas Mhor without your daddy.'

Melanie shuddered. 'It's gone.' She pointed to Ben Binnean, shrouded in thick mist. It was as if it had been spirited away.

Rachel smiled. 'It'll be there again when the mist clears.'

They donned jeans and wellingtons and set off. They met Ben on the way.

'Happy birthday, poppet,' he said, fishing in his duffle bag and bringing out a beautifully carved wooden rabbit. It was sitting in an alert, listening position and looked almost real. 'I know you like watching the bunnies, so I thought you'd like one of your own.

'Oh, thank you, Ben!' Melanie flung herself at him in delight. 'This is a lovely birthday!'

Even rain couldn't dampen Melanie's spirits, although they drove to Dunglevin and the cinema in a misty drizzle. It couldn't be much fun for Richard, fishing in weather like this, Rachel thought to herself.

Melanie enjoyed the film, laughing and crying and bouncing excitedly in her seat alternately, and afterwards they hurried through the rain to the Patisserie.

Richard wasn't there. They waited until five-thirty and then, because the café closed at six, they had their tea. It was a subdued little girl who ate a second slice of peach gateau.

'Daddy forgot,' she said, a large blob of cream clinging to her quivering lip.

'No, I'm sure he didn't. Something must have happened. The car's broken down—or something.' Rachel tried to sound convincing, but it was a sad, silent little Melanie who sat beside her on the drive home.

They had barely got inside the house when the phone rang. It was Richard.

'Can you send someone to pick me up at Ardenbeg,' he said tersely. He sounded tired and bad-tempered. 'I can't drive my car.'

'Melanie and I will fetch you,' said Rachel. She couldn't resist adding, 'We've only just got back from Dunglevin.'

There was a silence. 'Oh. Yes, of course. It's her birthday, isn't it.' He swore under his breath. 'I'll be waiting at the pierhead. How long do you think you'll be?'

'Ten minutes.' She put down the receiver.

'Daddy?' Melanie asked eagerly.

Rachel nodded. 'It sounds as if I was right. He wants us to fetch him, so his car must have broken down.'

They drove to Ardenbeg in thickening mist and found Richard leaning on a bollard at the pierhead.

His face was ashen and his hand was swathed in bandages.

'I'm sorry about your birthday tea, little one,' he said to Melanie as he wedged himself into the back seat of the Mini, 'but there's been a bit of an accident. I'll tell you about it later,' he added to Rachel. Then he leaned back and closed his eyes.

Back at Kilfinan House he went straight to his room. Rachel helped Melanie prepare for bed, parrying the little girl's questions with, 'We shall have to wait and see. No, I don't know what could have happened, we'll find out tomorrow, I'm sure.' She was just leaving Melanie when Richard came into the bedroom. His face had a trace more colour, Rachel noticed, but he looked haggard and drawn.

'I've brought your birthday present, Melanie,' he said. He handed her a small jewellers box. In it was a dainty gold cross and chain. 'I'm sorry it's so late, but at least it's still your birthday.'

Melanie opened it and her eyes shone with pleasure. She sat up in bed and held out her arms. 'It's lovely, Daddy. Thank you.' Smiling he bent down for her kiss, reeling a little as he stood up.

Rachel steadied him and helped him from the room, along to his study where he sank into a chair.

She poured him a stiff whisky, but he refused it. 'I think it's best not to mix alcohol with all the things the doctors have been pumping into me,' he said with a ghost of a smile, 'much though I should like one.'

Rachel sat down. 'What's happened, Richard?' she asked.

'I've lost my boat,' he said flatly.

'*Thursday's Child?*'

'No. *Celia*, the fishing boat.' He leaned back in his chair and closed his eyes. 'I suppose I should never have gone out today; it was overcast and I knew it could turn up foggy, but then there's always that possibility, and this party was coming over from Glasgow, and today was the only day they could come.' He sighed. 'So we went. It was all right until midday, then the fog closed in. It was as thick as a hedge. I was making for home, working by the charts and compass, and we'd got as far as Rubha Sgeir, which is a nasty, rocky little area as its name suggests, when this joker loomed on the port side and ran us down. It happened as quickly as I'm telling you, we didn't stand a chance. It was over almost in seconds.' He looked down at his bandaged hand. 'We were lucky—there were six of us in the boat and we all got away with nothing more than cuts and bruises. The boat that had rammed us picked us all up, but the *Celia* was pushed on to the rocks at Rubha Sgeir and broke her back and sank.' He passed his good hand over his face. 'So that's the end of another Celia.' His expression was desolate.

Rachel's heart went out to him. 'Was it insured?' she asked tentatively.

'Oh, yes. Everything was insured; boat, equipment, everything. But it was a stupid thing to happen,' he spoke impatiently. 'And it wasn't my fault. Well, it wasn't anybody's fault really, I suppose. Just one of those things.' He got up. 'I think I'll go to bed. I can break the news to my father in the morning, that'll be time enough to tell him. I can't do much with this damn thing.' He held up his hand. 'My right hand, too.'

Rachel left him, feeling helpless and inadequate. But she had barely reached her room when there was a knock at the door. Richard stood there. 'I'm sorry,' he said, 'could you ...?' He held out his good arm for her to undo the cuff button on his shirt. 'I always keep a change of clothing at the office,' he explained, 'so I was able to get into dry things as soon as we came ashore. The doctor who stitched my hand buttoned me up then.'

Rachel unbuttoned his cuff and he shook it loose and fumbled with the buttons on his shirt front. 'Oh, hell, I feel so bloody useless! I can't do a thing with my left hand—I never could.'

Deftly, Rachel unbuttoned the rest of his shirt, carefully keeping her eyes averted from his face. He must never know how she longed to put her arms round him and comfort him. 'There,' she said with a slight catch in her breath. 'Can you manage now?'

He swayed towards her, then recovered himself. 'Yes, thank you, I can manage now.' He smiled ruefully. 'I may need buttoning up in the morning, though.'

Over breakfast next morning Richard told Alistair about the distaster, whilst Melanie looked on, wide-eyed and silent. Rachel noticed that he had pulled on a roll-neck sweater so he had no need to come to her to be 'buttoned-up'.

Alistair listened gravely to the story, then asked, as Rachel had done, whether the boat had been adequately insured.

'Yes. But it'll take some time to come through. You know what these things are.'

'So what are you going to do in the meantime?'

'Can't do anything until this heals.' Richard indicated his bandaged hand, ineptly chasing a piece of sausage round his plate with his left hand as he spoke.

'And then?'

Richard shrugged. 'Start again, I suppose.'

'That won't be for three or four months, though, will it?' Alistair's gaze was intent.

'Probably not until the spring. By the time everything's sorted out it'll be Christmas—not much point in starting then till the weather improves and the holidaymakers come. I don't know. I'll see. Right now, I'm fed up with the whole business.'

'Hm.' Alistair wiped his mouth with his napkin. 'Rose will be coming home soon,' he said, changing the subject.

'That'll make two semi-invalids around the place,' commented Richard, with a trace of bitterness.

Alistair ignored that remark. 'I've been turning over in my mind the possibility of Rose going away somewhere to convalesce.' He reached for toast and marmalade as he spoke.

'I'm sure that would do her a world of good,' Rachel said warmly. 'And I know my family would be delighted to have her to stay. They haven't seen each other for years.'

'I was thinking of something a little more ... well, exciting is perhaps the word, than that.' Alistair's voice was almost diffident.

'Like what?' Richard asked with a somewhat cynical smile. 'A world cruise?'

'Well, yes, something like that. A Mediterranean cruise, anyway.'

Richard and Rachel both regarded him with amazement. Melanie had slipped unnoticed out of the room some time back.

'Don't you think she'd like that?' Alistair asked.

'I'm sure she would,' Rachel replied. 'But....'

'But what?'

'I expect she'd like it more if someone went with her,' Richard said, voicing Rachel's thoughts.

'But I'd no intention of letting her go alone,' Alistair said mildly.

'Rachel can't go,' said Richard, quickly. 'There's Melanie....'

No, Rachel thought wretchedly, Melanie's governess can't be spared. But only because she is Melanie's governess.

'I hadn't thought of Rachel.' Alistair hesitated. 'In fact, if you would be prepared to manage the Estate for me, Richard, I rather thought I might go myself.'

Nobody spoke at this bombshell.

'I've never been to Greece or Crete or any of those places,' Alistair went on, 'and I'd very much like to before I get too old. Of course, I've been to North Africa. I was there during the war and have a souvenir to prove it.' He patted his lame leg. 'I've thought about this a lot, but couldn't see how I could leave the Estate; Ben obviously couldn't manage it alone.... But now this has happened.' He spread his hands. 'It could all work out very well, Richard.'

Richard snorted and rested his arm gingerly on the table. 'At the moment I don't feel capable of managing anything, I'll tell you that,' he said. 'This thing's damned painful. I didn't sleep a wink last night.'

Alistair got up from the table. 'Well, you've got time to think it over, Richard,' he said. 'I won't say anything to Rose until you've made your decision.'

'Crafty old so-and-so!' Richard muttered as Alistair closed the door behind him. 'He knows perfectly well he'll get his own way. He nearly always does.' But he was smiling.

CHAPTER TEN

RICHARD took the loss of his boat more philosophically than Rachel had expected. He fumed at the pain and inconvenience of his injured hand, and particularly at his inability to drive his car, but Alistair kept him too busy to brood, occupying his time either in the office or roaming the Estate with Ben. It seemed to Rachel that Alistair was going to make sure that Richard could run things competently in his absence.

As for Rose, excitement at the prospect of a cruise drove everything else from her mind and brought colour to her cheeks. Rachel was kept on her toes shopping and packing for her, and she lost count of the number of phone calls she had from her aunt. 'Did I put sun-tan oil on my list? And I'd better take some seasickness pills, just in case.' Another time, 'Do you really think you should buy me trousers, my girl? I've never worn them before. Perhaps I'm too old.'

Rachel couldn't help laughing. 'Of course you're not too old, Auntie. Everyone wears trousers these days. By the way, I can't find the blue blouse you wanted. I can find a pink one. . . .'

'Oh, never mind, get me a new one when you come to Dunglevin next time. After all, a trip like this only happens once in a lifetime.' And so it went on.

But at last everything was ready, trunks packed and piled in the hall at Kilfinan House, and Alistair fetched Rose from hospital ready for leaving the following day.

Rachel took her aunt a bedtime drink. Rose had in-

sisted on spending the night in her own cottage, so
Rachel was there, too, keeping her company.

'I feel as if I've been away for years.' Rose accepted
her drink gratefully. 'So much seems to have happened
—poor Richard losing his boat like that. He'd had
such hopes for that boat, you know. And Melanie....'
Her face softened at the recollection of Melanie's greeting, the delighted shriek of 'Rose!' and the bear-hug
which Rose had, for once, found no difficulty in returning. It was a new, mellow Rose who had come
home.

She looked at Rachel over the rim of her mug.
'You've done wonders with that child, my girl. What's
your secret?'

'Love and patience.' Rachel sat on the side of the bed,
a frown creasing her brow. 'Melanie has certainly made
great strides. She talks much more now in that funny,
slow way she has, but she's becoming quite articulate.
There's still something, some barrier, though.... I
don't know what it is. I just feel, somehow, that something still bothers her.' She shrugged. 'Maybe it's just
my imagination. Tell me, Auntie, how much do you
think Melanie misses her mother?'

Rose finished her drink and set the mug down on the
table beside her bed. 'I never liked Richard's wife,'
she said carefully. 'I know people thought I was simply
jealous, that whoever Richard married I would have
resented because I was his nanny and he was my boy,
I'd brought him up.' She shook her head. 'That wasn't
true. I would have—still would—like nothing better
than to see him happily married. But to see the way
that woman carried on with other men behind his
back....' She sighed. 'Oh, Celia was very discreet. Not
many people were aware of what was going on; I don't
think Alistair suspects even to this day. But I knew.'

She gave a wry smile. 'When Melanie was born I think Celia realised she'd been a bit hasty in moving me to this cottage. I would have been so much more useful on the spot. But I refused to go back, even though she asked me. A child was an encumbrance to her. She'd never wanted children at all, you see.'

'Richard did?'

Rose smiled. 'Oh, yes. Richard wanted a son. Even so, I remember him coming to me the day Melanie was born. "She's beautiful, Rose," he said. "A real Duncan." "And what about the son you were so set on having?" I teased him. "Plenty of time for that. We'll have a son next time," he said. Only there wasn't a next time, was there?' Rose shook her head sadly.

She still hadn't answered Rachel's question. 'Do you think Melanie misses Celia?' she repeated.

Rose bit her lip. 'If the accident had happened three months earlier I would have said no,' she replied. 'The child spent more time with me than anybody up until then. But in the last three months it was different.' She paused. 'That was when Celia started going out in the daytime as well as at night. I suppose she took the child with her as a cover, so that people wouldn't suspect what was going on. Sometimes she went on foot, sometimes by car, but she was always going to the same place. She couldn't leave the man alone.'

'What man?' But Rachel knew what her aunt would say.

'Why, Ben Carson, of course.'

Lying in her bed under the eaves at Rose's cottage Rachel went over the conversation she had had with her aunt. It all sounded so plausible—not at all the rantings of an old woman deranged by jealousy as Ben had suggested. And Melanie knew Ben very well, was clearly fond of him and at ease in his company, a relationship compatible with her having spent a good deal of time in his presence. But Ben had been the one person who had never encouraged Melanie to talk—in fact, had almost discouraged her. Almost as if he was afraid that if she spoke she might say too much. . . . He made no secret of his admiration for Richard's wife, either. Strangely, it was this last fact that made Rachel uneasy. A man having an affair with another man's wife would hardly boast of his attraction towards her.

It was very late before Rachel slept.

The next day was Saturday and the whole household assembled to see Rose and Alistair off on the first leg of their journey. Richard's hand was not sufficiently recovered to drive long distances, so Ben was going to take them as far as Glasgow. Rose looked very smart in a practical navy trouser suit and Alistair hovered round her, helping her into the car and tucking a rug round her.

'You'd think they were off on their honeymoon!' Richard whispered to Rachel, with a grin, as they waved them down the drive, Melanie beside them, hopping ecstatically from one foot to the other. Mrs Munroe wiped her eye on the corner of her apron and hurried back to the kitchen.

'Would you like some more coffee?' Richard asked Rachel. He seemed reluctant to let her go, for some reason.

'It's probably cold by now.' As it was Saturday she had no special plans, Melanie had gone off to find Mrs Munroe's Jeannie. She followed him back to the dining room, where Mrs Munroe had begun to clear the table, and put her hand on the coffee pot.

'Och, I'll mak' some fresh, it'll no tak' a sec,' Mrs Munroe volunteered, whisking it away.

Rachel sat down at the table and Richard sat opposite, flexing his hand. The bandages were off now but the fingers were still swollen and marked and there was an ugly scar running across the palm. 'I'm getting more mobility into it,' he said, looking down at his sausage-like fingers, 'but it's very slow progress.' He was wearing denim jeans, a thin sweater and an unzipped leather lumber jacket. It struck Rachel, not for the first time, that Richard Duncan would look distinguished whatever he wore.

'The doctors said you were lucky not to lose some fingers,' she reminded him. 'But you didn't. They're all there and eventually they'll all work again. You must just be patient.'

He sighed. 'Yes, I suppose you're right. I'm getting quite adept at writing with my left hand, though.'

Mrs Munroe brought in the coffee on a tray and put it in front of Rachel.

Richard stared at the big chased silver coffee pot. 'You know, this whole place is a white elephant,' he said sadly. 'Until I started going through things with my father I simply hadn't realised.... There's all this land, the house, furniture, paintings, all worth a fortune. But no money. Periodically, my father has to sell something—a painting, a piece of land, something like that, to keep things going. I don't know which painting has gone to pay for this cruise, he wouldn't say, but I know he's had to sell one.' He accepted a cup of coffee from Rachel and his fingers brushed hers, sending the familiar tingle through her veins and making it difficult for her to concentrate on his words.

'You can't keep on selling off family heirlooms in order to live,' he went on, 'it's all wrong; you end up with nothing at all. A place this size should be made to work for itself. I know what could be done ...' he shook his head, 'but of course Alistair would never agree.'

'I suppose,' Rachel sipped her coffee thoughtfully, 'this could be the reason he was so against Melanie going to boarding school. The fees would have been yet another drain.'

Richard nodded. 'And as it was a special private school the fees were very high. Yes, I'm sure you're right about that, but of course, he'd never admit it.' He made an impatient gesture. 'Why on earth didn't he *say* what was happening? After all, I am his son!'

'Perhaps he thought you weren't interested,' said Rachel, tracing the design on the handle of the coffee pot with her finger. 'I remember you telling me once that you found it impossible to work with him.'

His shoulders sagged. 'Yes, I suppose I am partly to blame. But he would never listen to my ideas.' He finished his coffee and got up and began to wander round the room. 'Things have got to such a state now, though, that something's got to be done. The whole Estate's running down. I'd no idea until I went over it with him and Ben. There's far too much for Ben to cope with alone, too.' He came and leaned on the back of a chair. 'But there are several things that we could do, just for starters.' He ticked them off on the fingers of his good hand. 'We could easily support twice as many sheep as we've got. We've endless grazing and it's virtually going to waste. Some of the small cottages dotted around could be done up and let out as holiday cottages, or even sold as such.' He gazed round the room. 'We could even turn this place into an hotel—goodness knows it's big enough, and we don't actually live in a quarter of the space. . . .'

Rachel smiled. 'I don't think Alistair would ever agree to that.'

'No, perhaps you're right. I got a bit carried away. But we could sell the fishing rights in the river. There's salmon and brown trout.... Oh, heavens, a place this size *must* be made to pay!' He went to the door. 'If only the old man would give me a free hand, *I'd* make it pay,' he added as he reached it.

Rachel's heart went out to him, but she knew there was no way she could help him. Unless.... Melanie was much better now, one might say, back to normal. What she needed more than anything was the company of other children. School was the obvious answer. Not the special school Richard had had in mind when Rachel arrived at Glencarrick but an ordinary school, such as the other children in the Glen attended. This was at Ardenbeg. There were even facilities for children to board for the week, coming home at week-ends. It would be ideal for Melanie and it would mean she would no longer need a governess. She, Rachel, could return home. Home. She realised suddenly that she had come to regard Kilfinan House as home, and that would never do. It would seem that the sooner she made plans to return to Suffolk the better.

After lunch, with Mrs Munroe and Jeannie gone home and Richard off to a far corner of the Estate with Ben, Rachel suggested a ride and a walk to Melanie.

'And I know just where we'll go,' she added mysteriously, much to Melanie's delight.

But when she drove the car through Ardenbeg and along the high road by the loch, pulling in at the vantage point above Eilean Dorcha, Melanie began to whimper. 'Not here. Please not here!' She clutched Rachel's hand.

Rachel put her arm round the little girl's shoulders. 'Now, why not, Melanie? What are you afraid of?

I've brought you to this place several times purposely to show you that there's nothing for you to fear. So why are you still worried about it?'

'Long way down.' Melanie shuddered.

'Yes, but there's a footpath. Come with me, I'll show you.'

'No. Get lost! Leave me!'

'Of course you won't get lost. And of course I shan't leave you.' Rachel studied the child. Her eyes were big with fear and her speech had reverted almost to monosyllables. There was obviously something about this particular spot that terrified Melanie still. Or rather the memory of something here. Rachel sat quietly in the car with her arm encircling the little body.

'You've been here before, then?'

A violent nod.

'Who did you come with?'

'You.'

'No, before you came with me. Did you come with Rose? Grandpa? Daddy? Ben?' She hesitated between each one. 'Mummy?'

'Yes.' It was barely more than a whisper.

'Mummy. You came here for a walk with your mummy.'

Melanie nodded, her little body was tense.

'That was nice.' Rachel kept her voice soothing. Melanie had never before mentioned her mother. 'Would you like to tell me about it? Perhaps you could show me where you went.'

'No. Got lost.' Melanie was shivering. 'All alone.'

Rachel got out of the car and walked round to Melanie's side. By the time she opened the door the little girl was curled up in a ball with her arm across her face. Rachel was completely baffled. But she knew without any doubt that here, at this place, lay the reason for Melanie's strange behaviour. If only she would talk about it!

'Now come along, darling,' she coaxed, 'show me where you went. I promise you won't be alone. We'll hold hands all the way.' As she spoke she was gently easing Melanie out of the car and leading her to the stile. 'We'll go this way, shall we?' Talking to her and holding firmly on to her hand, Rachel led the reluctant little girl along the forest trail, down rough-hewn steps and along overgrown pathways. Once they came unexpectedly to a tiny lake with the remains of waterlilies in it and an ornate stone bridge by a little waterfall, and Rachel remembered that Ben had once told her that at one time there had been a castle at the edge of the loch near Eilean Dorcha, so this must be the remains of its landscape garden. She spoke of this to Melanie, but Melanie didn't answer, she might not even have heard, and her hand in Rachel's was cold and clammy.

Quite suddenly they came to a clearing. Heaps of stones and a low rectangle of wall was all that was left to show that here had stood the castle that Ben had spoken of.

Melanie began to cry.

Rachel sat down with her on a mound of tussocky grass and let her cry for a while. She could see just below her the dark shape of Eilean Dorcha against the blue of the loch and the boats moored in its shelter. From this distance the little lighthouse looked like a toy model. Gulls wheeled and shrieked in the sky, but that and Melanie's sobs were all that disturbed the air.

'Now,' Rachel said, when at last the tears stopped, 'tell me all about it. Tell me everything, then it won't worry you any more, I promise you that.'

Melanie lifted a tear-stained face and Rachel detected a plea in the dark brown eyes.

'I'll help you. Tell me if I go wrong,' Rachel encouraged. 'Now, I think this is what happened. You came to the vantage point with Mummy, parked the car and walked—just like we've done today?'

An uncertain nod.

'You and Mummy became separated and then you couldn't find her at all?'

'They hurried. I couldn't keep up,' Melanie said in a halting whisper.

'They? There was someone else?'

Melanie nodded, biting her lip.

Rachel hesitated, undecided whether to press the child as to who the other person was, but decided against it for the moment and contented herself by prompting, 'But they found you. They waited for you and....'

Melanie shook her head emphatically. 'Here. Found them here. Kissing. Over there. Kissing and.... Mummy was cross.' Her voice dropped even further. 'Said I mustn't ever say.' She looked up at Rachel, her eyes beseeching. Rachel nodded and smiled at her, then suddenly, as if this was what she'd been waiting for, it all came out in a flood, the words tumbling over themselves as she opened her heart.

'I always went with them. They said it was secret, that I mustn't ever say, and that if I did something dreadful would happen. They often came here. Sometimes I'd have to stay in the car while they went somewhere. He was nice to me; he always gave me sweets. One day he gave me so many I was sick. I didn't like being alone in the car up here, I was afraid it would roll over the edge, but they gave me books to read and said I'd be all right. Sometimes Mummy would say

Oh, let her come, if I cried too much, but one day I got lost in the woods and I cried even more because I couldn't find them. And then I did, and they were here and they were kissing on the grass, and he was cross and he said never to speak of it or something really dreadful would happen.' She took a deep shuddering breath. 'I didn't speak of it, truly I didn't, not to *anybody*, not *ever*, Rachel, but something dreadful still happened.' She hesitated. 'Rachel, do you think the dreadful thing happened because I *thought* about it so much? Do you think it was my fault Mummy's car crashed?'

'Oh, Melanie, no!' Rachel gathered the little figure to her and held her close. 'You were never in any way to blame and you must never think you might have been. Your mother's car crashed because she took a bend too fast, it was purely an accident. It had nothing whatever to do with anything you may have thought or even said.' She gave the child a gentle shake. 'Do you understand, dear? It would have happened anyway. You couldn't possibly have influenced it, either consciously or unconsciously.' She paused. Melanie wouldn't understand those words. 'You couldn't have made it happen—even if you'd wanted to,' she finished.

'I didn't want to,' Melanie said seriously, 'but sometimes I almost wished she'd go away so I didn't have to keep so many secrets.' She was calmer now. She sat on Rachel's lap, her head nestled against her shoulder and Rachel held her close and stroked her hair. Here was the answer to Melanie's silence; quite simply, afraid of saying something she shouldn't, she subconsciously found it easier to say nothing at all. And it had taken these past months of patient affection, which for varying reasons the child had never received before, to pierce and finally shatter the barrier she had unwit-

tingly put up against the world. Poor little Melanie!
Rachel gazed down at her. She had fallen into an
exhausted sleep, her face streaked with tears, but
strangely serene and untroubled. It was as if a great
weight had been lifted from her shoulders—as indeed
it had. Rachel turned her eyes to the distant shore of
the loch, beyond Eilean Dorcha, to where the heather-
capped hills rose uneven against the sky. So Rose had
been right after all. Celia Duncan had been unfaithful to Richard and Ben had lied. No wonder he had
never encouraged Melanie to speak! Yet one thing
struck Rachel as rather odd. In Melanie's story of her
mother's affair, not once had she mentioned Ben by
name.

Melanie stirred. 'Come along, darling. Time to go
home,' Rachel said with a smile.

The little girl slid to the ground. 'I know the way.
Follow me.' She didn't even bother to hold Rachel's
hand as they climbed back to the road, and she prattled
happily all the way home in the car.

But Rachel was troubled. How much should she tell
Richard of Melanie's story? Something would have to
be said, the change in the child was so dramatic, but
how could she, of all people, be the one to shatter his
faith in his beloved Celia? On the one hand he would
never forgive her—if, indeed, he would even believe
her—and on the other it would surely send him straight
into Moira McLeod's waiting arms. She decided to
wait a few days until Richard commented on his
daughter's change of behaviour, which he surely would.

She was right. But it was almost a week later that he
knocked on her sitting room door about nine o'clock
in the evening. She had washed her hair and it was still
damp after towelling and brushing, so rather than get
out her hair-dryer she was sitting by the fire, reading.

'Don't get up.' He had opened the door and let himself in. He came and sat in the armchair opposite to her, dressed casually tonight, in grey slacks and a black shirt, open at the neck. Rachel noticed that his eyes were very blue against his deeply tanned face. He looked at her without smiling, automatically flexing his injured hand, a habit he had acquired lately. 'What's come over Melanie?' he asked. 'She's ...' he cast round for the right word, 'she's normal.' He sounded almost accusing.

'Aren't you pleased?' she stalled for time.

'Of course I'm pleased. But how did it happen? And, more to the point, will it last?'

Rachel leaned forward and pushed a curtain of hair away from her face. 'I think it will last,' she said slowly, 'now that we've discovered the cause. It was simply that she was frightened, too frightened to speak.'

'What was she afraid of, for goodness' sake?'

Rachel stole a glance at him. He was scowling. In spite of hours of thought she still wasn't sure how to explain Melanie's transformation to him without a downright lie. Yet how could she speak the truth without shattering his love and faith in his dead wife? This was something she knew she could never do.

'Well——' she hesitated for such a long time that he prompted, 'Well, go on,'

'Well,' she repeated, 'you know how scared she's always been of the vantage point on the road above the loch?'

She looked at him. His nod was barely perceptible, but his eyes never left her face.

'It seems—someone took her there and on the walk down the forest trail she somehow got lost. She was so frightened that....' Her voice trailed off. It didn't sound plausible, even to her own ears.

He gazed at her, his expression enigmatic. 'Come now, Rachel, you'll have to do better than that,' he said softly. Let's have the truth.'

'I—it is the truth.' But she was unable to meet his gaze.

'I'm sure it is, as far as it goes.' He leaned forward and took her chin in his hand, turning her face up so that she was forced to look at him. 'But there's more. There has to be more.' His expression now was stern.

Rachel licked her lips. 'I told you, she was frightened. She could never talk about it before because she felt insecure. But now....' She spoke breathlessly. His face was so close that she could feel his breath warm on her cheek.

'Yes. Now she's lucky enough to have you.' His hand left her chin and slid carelessly down her neck before he leaned back in his chair.

'She really needs the company of other children now. The school at Ardenbeg looks very suitable, Mrs Munroe's Jeannie goes there, so she would have a friend. She certainly doesn't need to go to a special school....' Rachel knew she was prattling, but she couldn't help it. Anything was better than letting him know the effect he had on her. And it was getting worse instead of better. Just to be near him....

'Melanie's education is not what we were discussing at the moment.' She realised he was speaking again. 'What I am asking for is an explanation of her sudden blossoming into,' again he hesitated over the word, 'normality.'

'Oh, it's not sudden. It's been coming for some time.'

'All right, it's been coming for some time. But all of a sudden it's arrived. How? Why? I want to know.' He was becoming impatient. He shifted in his chair. 'For a start, *who* took her to the forest trail and then was stupid enough to lose her?'

Rachel bent her head. 'She told me it was Celia, her mother,' she said in a low voice.

He nodded. 'I thought as much. And who else?'

'What do you mean?' Rachel pushed her hair back and looked up at him.

'Exactly what I say. Who else? Which man had my bitch of a wife got with her? Oh,' seeing the shocked expression on Rachel's face, 'do you think I didn't know? Do you imagine I was that blind?' He shook his head sadly, 'but I didn't think that even Celia would have been callous enough to involve an innocent child.' He was silent for a moment, staring at his injured hand. 'I named my fishing boat after Celia,' he mused. 'And do you know why?' His face twisted into a bitter smile as he looked up at Rachel.

She shook her head, too shattered to speak.

'Out of sheer bloody-mindedness, that's why. And she was furious. She'd never wanted me to have the boat in the first place. The idea of being married to a fisherman simply didn't have the appeal that being married to a gentleman farmer did—even if the gentleman farmer was only a "yes-man" to his father. She was a terrible snob, my wife. So I called it *Celia* just to spite her. It was aptly named, too, in a way. It attracted the men and it was fickle—just like her. I was glad to be rid of both of them,' Richard finished vehemently.

Rachel stared at him, too shocked to speak. She had never expected such an outburst from Richard Duncan.

'It could have been any one of a number of men that Melanie saw her with,' he went on cynically. 'Maybe she didn't even know who he was. Yet,' he frowned, 'towards the end Celia changed. I think there was someone. She'd even mentioned divorce. . . .'

'Ben Carson?' Rachel's voice was barely above a whisper.

He looked at her for a long time and Rachel felt the colour come into her cheeks. 'No, Rachel,' he said at last. 'Whoever it was it wasn't Ben Carson, so you have no need to worry about that.' He shrugged. 'Oh, he may have fancied himself in love with her, but Celia was no Lady Chatterley, amusing herself with the game-keeper. She liked her men to be rich and distinguished. When my wife sold herself the price was high. The slut!' His voice was full of loathing and disgust. 'She married me because I was heir to the biggest estate in the county. But one man was never enough for my wife.'

'And your reason for marrying her?' Rachel couldn't help asking.

'I was young, flattered by the attentions of a beauti-ful woman, and a stupid fool. It was the biggest mistake of my life and one I'm never, ever likely to repeat,' he added forcefully.

So, thought Rachel, that was the reason Miora Mc-Leod's advances had so far met with no success. It was not that he had been so in love with his wife that no other woman could take her place, but rather that having been taken in by a woman once he was not going to risk the same thing happening again. Once bitten, twice shy. And who could blame him?

He got up to go and she stood up with him.

'You don't really need to tell me any more,' he said with a sigh. 'I've no doubt that I can more or less piece the story together for myself. Celia was a callous crea-ture, with precious little love for the child.' He gazed at Rachel and his expression softened. 'I think you have far more love for my daughter than her mother ever had, Rachel,' he said quietly. He put out his hand

and gently touched her cheek, then he shook his head. 'But there must have been something pretty traumatic to rob her of her speech altogether.'

Rachel bit her lip. 'If she was told to keep a secret or something awful would happen,' she said slowly. 'Then she found that there were so many secrets to keep that she got confused as to what she might speak about and what she might not, she might subconsciously find it safer not to speak at all.'

He nodded. 'Yes, you could be right, at that.'

'Then something dreadful does happen—her mother is killed. She wonders if somehow she's to blame. Had she said something she shouldn't have? There's nobody she can confide in, so what does she do? She turns in on herself.', Rachel spoke jerkily, unhappy at having to say these things. 'That's how I see it, at any rate.'

'It sounds very plausible to me.' Richard passed his hand over his face, 'Thank you for, what shall I say? "unlocking her", Rachel.' He smiled his rare smile. 'I'm sure nobody else could have done it.' He paused. 'But now you think it's time she went to school?'

'I think it's time for her to begin to mix with other children. Yes, I think school's the answer.' Rachel knew she was signing her own death warrant, so to speak, for with Melanie at school and Rose back from her cruise there would be nothing to keep her at Kilfinan House. She would have to return to her home in Suffolk.

He regarded her thoughtfully. 'You're probably right,' he said. 'And no doubt you have plans of your own?'

She looked into the future, bleak without him, at empty years spent teaching other people's children. Somehow she managed to smile brightly. 'Oh, yes,' she replied, 'I've got plans of my own.'

CHAPTER ELEVEN

SEVERAL weeks went by. The trees turned from green to brown and the chill autumn mists covered the mountain tops for longer and longer. Letters from Alistair and Rose, telling of hot sunshine, orange groves and grape harvests, contrasted strongly with the roaring log fires that Ben built to cheer the cold Scottish evenings.

Gradually Rachel ceased to be shocked by what Richard had revealed of his feelings towards his wife. But she was puzzled.

Richard had insisted that Celia was not going to Ben Carson that night. Was this true? Was she going to someone else? Or had he simply said that to protect her, Rachel's feelings, thinking that she and Ben ...? Her face flamed at the memory of Richard's expression the day he had seen her come out of the bedroom at Rose's cottage with Ben.

She frowned. Yet if Celia *hadn't* been going to Ben why should Ben have bothered to cover himself by saying that her car crashed coming *back* from Dunglevin, when everyone else said she was going the other way? The whole affair was a complete mystery, a mystery deepened by the fact the story 'put about', as Rose described it, that Celia had been on her way to visit her sick mother was totally untrue; she didn't even have a mother.

A more sinister suspicion crept into Rachel's mind. Could Celia Duncan have been lured to her death? Someone who hated her and wanted her out of the way could easily have tampered with the steering on her car. On those treacherous bends on the high road above the loch anything might happen.... But who? Rachel closed her eyes to try and shut out the image that came to her mind. No, surely Richard hadn't hated his wife enough to do a thing like that!

But even these disturbing thoughts were pushed to the back of her mind by a letter that came from Alistair and Rose. It was from Athens. Richard opened it at the breakfast table and read it through twice without speaking. Then he handed it to Rachel, still without comment.

Rachel began to read Alistair's neat, carefully looped script. The letter began by describing the scenery and customs of the places they had recently visited, as Alistair's letter usually did, but then it went on:

'Rose and I were married this morning, very quietly. You may be surprised at this, but I think probably you will not; we have been friends for such a very long time. We are very happy and wonder now why we have never got round to it before. I hope we shall have many years to enjoy each other's company.

'Which brings me to another point. I think it's time I handed the reins over to you, Richard. The Estate is less prosperous than it should be, for a number of reasons, but with your vision and drive and a free hand to run it as you choose I'm sure you will make a success of it. I only wish you had a wife to share the responsibilities and joys of it all (Kilfinan House can be a very real joy, I assure you, although it seems a very long time since it was anything but a burden to me. Perhaps I am growing old). But I'm hopeful. I've seen small signs that encourage me to think that you are considering remarriage and I would like to say now that your choice has my full approval.

'But I'm being precipitate. To be more down-to-earth, Rose and I have decided that Arden Lodge, on the far side of the Estate, will suit us very well. It is bigger than Kilfinan Cottage, yet not too big; it is also further away from Kilfinan House, so your activities will not be constantly under my scrutiny—important, I feel, for both our sakes. Rose and I will not be returning home for another month, time enough for Ben to check things over and do any redecorating necessary. Both Rose and I are happy to leave colour schemes etc. to Rachel. She has excellent taste.' He signed the letter rather formally, 'Your affectionate father, Alistair Duncan.'

Rachel handed the letter back to Richard, her feelings mixed.

'He's right. I'm not really surprised they've got married, are you?' Richard glanced at her as he spoke.

'No, not really.' Rachel stirred her coffee thoughtfully. 'He seems to be assuming rather a lot, though. Of you, I mean.' She spoke slowly.

'You mean dumping the Estate on me?' Richard smiled wryly. 'Rachel, my father knows me almost as well as I know myself, although we may not appear to be very close. He knows I like nothing better than a challenge. He also knows I need a free hand, so he's offering me both.' He traced patterns in the sugar bowl with a spoon. 'He's watched me trying to build my fishing business in Ardenbeg, never offering help or advice. It's been a slow job for me, paying off mortgages, replacing tackle, keeping the boat seaworthy and at the same time trying to make a profit. This year would have been the first really successful season. But,' he shrugged, 'there it is. At least we'll have the insurance money to help put Kilfinan on its feet again.'

'You'll miss fishing.'

'I'll still have *Thursday's Child*. I just shan't do anything on a commercial basis.' He got up from his chair. 'I'm very happy with the way my father has planned everything. I couldn't have organised it better myself. He's a shrewd old devil, there's no doubt about that. He doesn't miss a trick.' His eyes rested on her for a moment. 'At least, not very often.' He went to the door. 'Perhaps you'd care to come over to Arden Lodge with me some time and see what needs to be done, these things need a woman's eye. Then you can talk it over with Ben. You'll enjoy that.' There was a hint of sarcasm in his tone.

He left the room and Rachel remained seated at the table, re-reading Alistair's letter. The words 'I've seen small signs that encourage me to think you are considering remarriage.... Your choice has my full approval' seemed to leap out of the page at her. Yes, of course Alistair would approve; an amalgamation of the Kilfinan Estate with the prosperous McLeod Farm could be nothing but an advantage to the Duncans, and Moira's hard-headed business acumen was just what was needed. Moira McLeod would make a perfect daughter-in-law as far as Alistair was concerned.

'You're very late coming to lessons this morning, Rachel. I've been in the playroom simply ages waiting for you.' Melanie came skipping into the room, her thick hair bouncing and her eyes alight with happiness. She seemed to blossom more with each succeeding day. 'Look, I've been drawing you a picture while I waited.' She spread a paper on the table in front of Rachel, carefully pushing aside coffee cups, the sugar bowl and marmalade dish to make room. 'Jeannie says that's how they sit in school.' She had drawn her impression of a classroom, crowded with stick-like children, the teacher at the front, an almost recognisable caricature of Rachel with long yellow hair, her arm round a little girl who looked not unlike Melanie herself.

'Would you like to go to school?' Rachel asked.

Melanie put her head on one side. 'Jeannie says it's fun. They play all sorts of games and do lots of lovely things. I think I'd like it.' She nodded. 'Yes, I'd like to go to school with Jeannie. Can I go soon?'

'Not until you've learned to spell a bit better,' Rachel managed to smile as she spoke. 'Come on, up to the playroom. Let's start work!' She patted Melanie's bottom to gee her up and followed her up the stairs with a heavy heart. Everything was falling neatly into place, too neatly, in fact. With Rose and Alistair married and moving to Arden Lodge; Richard taking over the running of the estate, married to Moira, a hard-headed business woman as well as a wife; and Melanie safely and happily settled at school, where did that leave her? She sighed. She had come to Glencarrick to recover from the shock of Keith's death. This she had done. Keith would always have a place in her memory, but the thought of him no longer hurt. So the purpose of her visit fulfilled, surely she should be ready to go home to Suffolk. Yet her heart was even heavier now than when she had arrived, all those months ago. Why? Damn Richard Duncan, she said to herself vehemently. She wished she had never met him.

Nevertheless, she accompanied him to Arden Lodge one grey October day. It was a two-mile drive along a bumpy cart track round the foot of the mountain. 'It's smoother by road,' he told her, clutching the steering wheel to avoid having it wrenched out of his hand, 'but about three times as far. We shan't see an awful lot of Rose and Alistair when they move here.'

'By that time I daresay I'll be gone,' Rachel commented.

'So soon?' A look, almost of alarm, crossed his face.

'Not until Melanie is settled at school, of course.'

'That may not be until after Christmas.' He kept his eyes on the road. 'There are other things to be considered. Whether or not she should board, for instance.... Ah, here we are.'

He pulled up outside a two-storied, double-fronted lodge, almost twice the size of Rose's cottage on the Glencarrick Road, and they went inside.

'It's very nice,' said Rachel, walking through the rooms. 'In reasonably good order, too. And centrally heated. I didn't expect that.'

'Yes. It's not been vacant all that long. A man by the name of Batchelor, he was a bachelor, too, used to live here. Kept himself very much to himself. Strange man, about my age, I should think. Often used to see him wandering over the hills. He left, oh, I don't know—not long before you came, I should think.'

They wandered from room to room making notes of things to be done. When they had finished Richard leaned his elbows on the landing banister and stood looking down into the hall.

'Ideal spot there for a grandfather clock. There, between those two doors, wouldn't you say?'

'Yes.' Rachel went and stood beside him. 'And I can picture a low chest with a copper jug full of flowers standing on it, there, opposite the front door.'

'Have you been up to the attics in Kilfinan House?'

She shook her head.

'You should. You'll find enough furniture stored up there to furnish this place three times over. All antique, of course.' He rubbed his chin. 'Come to think of it, there's another untapped source of revenue in those attics; some of the things up there could be quite valuable.'

'And quite useful for furnishing the cottages you're intending to rent out.'

'Mm. Yes, that's a thought. We can't have it both ways, can we?' He turned and walked into one of the bedrooms, commanding a view of Ben Binnean from the other side, a craggier, less kind aspect of the mountain. 'From the tone of his letter my father seems to think it's time I thought about marrying again,' he said over his shoulder. 'Do you think it would be a good idea?'

Rachel remained staring down into the empty hall, almost frozen. The thought of Richard and Moira married gave her an almost physical pain.

He returned to her side, leaning over the banister, and she felt the familiar thrill of his touch as his shoulder brushed hers.

'I. . . .' the words stuck in her throat. 'Not unless you're quite sure it's the right thing to do,' she said lamely.

'Melanie needs a mother. I can see that.'

Rachel was silent. Somehow she couldn't see Moira McLeod mothering a child of her own, let alone someone else's.

Richard sighed. 'But I need to be sure. . . .'

'It wouldn't be right for you to marry simply to provide a mother for Melanie,' she said carefully, keeping her eyes averted so he shouldn't see the pain in them.

'Many successful marriages have been built on less.'

'And many have failed on more.'

'There are other considerations.' He turned to face her, his deep-set eyes searching her face anxiously. 'Could you marry someone you didn't love, Rachel?' he asked. 'If there were very good reasons why you should?'

Rachel understood. It was the final humiliation. The

man she loved asking advice on whether he should marry someone else: Moira McLeod, the rich, shrewd businesswoman who would be such an asset to the Kilfinan Estate.

He gripped her arm. 'Well?' he asked, and there seemed to be a note almost of desperation in his voice. 'Could you?'

She shook her head. 'No,' she said wretchedly, 'never.'

He let her go abruptly and turned away. 'There's not an awful lot for Ben to do here,' he said, with a complete change of mood. 'The window frame in the small bedroom and the lock on the back door both need looking at; but apart from that and a washer on the kitchen tap the place is pretty well ready to furnish.'

'I think the lounge could do with redecorating.' Rachel tried to match his change of mood.

'Let's have another look.' He went down the stairs and into the lounge. 'Mm. Perhaps you're right.'

'I'm sure Ben won't mind doing it if I help him.' Rachel rubbed a faded patch on the wallpaper.

'No, I'm quite sure he won't.' There was a sarcastic twist to Richard's mouth. 'In fact, he'd probably be quite happy to redecorate the whole house—with your help.'

'What do you mean by that?'

He looked at her and his eyes now were hard and almost cruel. 'I mean that this place is far enough from the madding crowd for you to come here undisturbed ... whatever you might wish to do.'

'And if we come here to redecorate what else do you imagine we'll be doing?' Rachel was stung to reply.

'It's none of my business *what* you do,' he said coldly. 'As long as it's not under my nose.' There was no mistaking his insinuation. 'Of course, it won't be as comfortable as Rose's bedroom. . . .'

'How dare you!' Rachel raised her hand to strike him, but he caught it in a vice-like grip and twisted it behind her back, forcing her close to him. He held her like that for a moment, his face very close to hers. Then he muttered, 'I don't see why Ben should have it all,' and his mouth came down crushingly cruel on hers.

For a second she allowed herself to succumb to his kiss. This was what she had dreamed of so long and often, and the reality was no less than the dream. Helplessly, she found herself answering his demand. But then sanity prevailed and the full implication of his action hit her. She struggled with all her strength to free herself from Richard's grasp, but she was no match for him. But at last he released her and even he was breathless from the struggle. Without a word he left the house and she followed, but when he held open the door of the Range Rover for her to get in she said icily, 'Thank you, I'll walk back.'

'As you choose.' He got in and drove off at such a speed that the dust rose in clouds behind him.

Rachel walked home slowly. The way was rough and stony and when she was less than halfway a light drizzle began to fall. It matched her mood. She knew that Richard had been thinking of the day he had seen her leave the bedroom in Rose's cottage with Ben, speaking the way he had. She had never been able to explain to him the truth of that situation. At first she had been too embarrassed, then, seeing him locked in a passionate embrace with Moira that evening after the dinner party, she realised that it wasn't necessary. Let him think what he liked. It didn't matter. She simply didn't care. She was telling herself this yet again as she walked up the drive to Kilfinan House. She was, by this time, tired, chilled and bedraggled, and it didn't help that Richard passed her in his car on his way out. He didn't lift his hand in recognition, but she wouldn't have returned the salutation if he had.

Ben began work on Arden Lodge. After a week it was ready for carpeting and after two weeks it could be furnished. Rose had written full instructions as to which of the pieces she wanted from her cottage; Alistair wanted the desk from his study, but apart from that Rachel had a free hand. Ben helped her to select suitable items from the vast hoard in the attics at Kilfinan House.

'You could start an antique shop with this lot,' Ben remarked.

'It would be rather an out-of-the-way shop. Anyway, it'll be needed if Richard is going to furnish holiday cottages.' Rachel heaved a table out of her way. 'How many cottages are there, Ben?'

'Six. No, seven, including Rose's. She won't need hers now, will she?' Ben held up a chair. 'There are four of these dining chairs. Will they go with the table you've chosen?'

'Yes, they'll be just right. Like everything else they'll need a good polish. Everything's covered in dust.'

'Even your nose.' Ben flicked a speck of dust from her face. 'You know, Rachel, we should get married,' he said, his face serious. 'We get on very well together, don't we?'

Rachel smiled gently. 'Oh, Ben, you are a dear! I must say that's the funniest proposal I've ever had!'

'Well, what do you want me to do? Get down on one knee? There's not much room just here.' He looked round for a suitable space.

'Getting on well together isn't enough, is it, Ben?' She spoke seriously. 'Not for marriage.'

'It's better than nothing.'

'Maybe. But it's still not enough, although it's all we've got to offer each other.'

'Still Keith?' Ben touched her cheek.

At the gentle gesture her eyes filled with tears and she turned away. How little he knew! 'Come on,' she said, without answering his question, 'we'll never get this job done standing around.'

He took the hint and began hauling out a large sideboard. 'Well, if you don't get a better offer remember there's always old Ben in the background,' he said in an attempt to be lighthearted.

'You're a dear, Ben, but I don't think I shall. I'll be going back home to Suffolk soon.'

'When?'

'As soon as Rose and Alistair come back, I should think. Melanie should be settled at school by then, so I'll be needing to look for another job.'

'You've certainly worked wonders with her. I never ever thought she'd attend a normal school.'

'She's very anxious to go. Mrs Munroe's Jeannie goes and she's told Melanie all about it. Now Melanie is so keen to begin that Richard has been to see the headmaster and she starts next week, although it's midway through a term. She's very excited.'

It was an excitement that increased as the day drew near. Melanie's new dark green uniform was hung in her wardrobe and several times Rachel found signs that a dress rehearsal had been held.

At last the great day arrived.

'You look very smart, darling. Now don't let me down by having forgotten all I've taught you, will you?' Rachel teased to cover the lump in her throat.

'What are you going to do while I'm at school, Rachel?' Melanie regarded Rachel with her head on one side.

'I'm going to Arden Lodge. There are one or two more jobs to be done so that it will be ready for Rose and your grandfather.'

Melanie frowned. 'What will you do then?'

'Probably come and meet you from school.'

'No, I mean when Arden Lodge is done and Rose and Grandfather are home.'

'I don't know. I haven't thought about it,' Rachel lied. 'Now, off with you. Look, Daddy's waiting to take you to school.'

'Ready, little one?' Richard came into the room. He was wearing a suit as befitted such a special occasion. He nodded curtly to Rachel. Since that day at Arden Lodge they had maintained an icy politeness towards each other and Rachel was beginning to feel that she was winning her battle and that she heartily disliked the man.

'Yes, I'm ready, Daddy. Do I look nice?' Melanie pirouetted happily in front of him.

'*Very* smart. My word, you're growing up! Well, come along. Mustn't be late.'

'Aren't you coming, Rachel?' Melanie asked, holding her face up for a kiss.

'No. I've a bit more to do at Arden Lodge. Good-bye now, and good luck. Have a lovely day.'

Melanie ran ahead. At the door Richard turned. 'Oh, a message from Ben. He says he's ready when you are.' His voice was carefully flat.

'Thank you.' Rachel picked up her bag. 'I'm ready now.'

She followed him out of the house and waved to Melanie as he drove her off to school. Then she got into the truck with Ben and they went in the other direction towards Arden Lodge.

The Lodge was almost finished now. All the carpets were laid and some of the curtains were already hung.

Each time they went they took some furniture, so the rooms were gradually taking on a homely look.

Ben parked the truck by the back door and they carried in some chairs and pictures that had come from Kilfinan House and some hanging bookshelves that had come from Rose's cottage.

Towards the middle of the morning Ben was fixing a curtain rail in the little bedroom at the head of the stairs while Rachel fixed the hooks on to the curtains when the front door opened and they heard voices. Rachel went to the head of the stairs to see who was there and was just in time to see Richard and Moira walk into the lounge. She went back to Ben.

'It's only Richard. Looks as if he's brought Moira over to show her what's been done here.' Rachel sat on the bed and resumed her task.

'More likely Moira insisted on coming. She's a forceful character, Moira McLeod,' Ben remarked.

'....all very cosy,' Moira's voice floated up to them as she and Richard came out of the lounge and into the hall. 'Oh, that's a nice touch, that copper jug of chrysanthemums on that chest.'

Rachel knew she was referring to the chest opposite the front door which looked exactly as she had invisaged it would.

'That was Rachel's idea,' Richard's deep voice carried clearly up the stairs.

Their voices faded as they went into the dining room.

'I'm not surprised her brother went off to London.' Ben finished putting the last screw in and climbed down the step ladder. 'I should think he was glad to get away from her.'

'....nothing to prevent us being married now, is there?'

Rachel froze as Moira's voice came from the hall.

'It's all working out very nicely, Rick, isn't it? Alistair and Rose married and nicely tucked away here; the child at school—don't you really think she would be better boarding, darling—that leaves us free to run Kilfinan in conjunction with my place.'

'You seem to have got it all neatly planned,' Rachel heard Richard say, 'but you seem to have overlooked one thing.'

'Rachel?' said Moira. 'She'll go back where she came from, won't she? That doesn't concern us at all. After all, she only stayed on to look after Melanie after her aunt had the accident. She'll probably be glad to leave.'

Rachel looked at Ben. She hated eavesdropping like this, and so, from his expression, did Ben, but there was no way out of the bedroom except down the stairs, and it seemed from their voices that Richard and Moira were standing at the foot.

'I wasn't thinking of Rachel,' Richard was speaking now. 'No, what you seem to have overlooked, Moira, is the fact that I'm not in love with you. I have no intention of marrying you ...' he hesitated '... or anybody else, for that matter. I'm sorry, Moira, if you thought differently, but—well, there it is.'

'You're not *still* moping after Celia!' Moira's voice was full of scorn. 'Surely even you couldn't be so naïve? Don't you realise what she was like? Didn't you know about her men friends?' Her voice rose higher and higher. 'Didn't you know about her and my brother David?' Her voice dropped, but only slightly. 'She went to meet him in Dunglevin the night she was killed. His idea was to have a farewell drink before going to London the next day, but she had different ideas. She'd got a suitcase with her and she was all ready to go with him. She pleaded with him to take

her, went down on her knees, David told me afterwards
—he said it was quite embarrassing.' Moira gave an
ugly little laugh. 'Do you realise the implications,
Richard? *Your* wife pleaded with my brother to take
her away with him. Where did you fall short as a
husband, I ask myself, that your wife should do that,
knowing that David was only interested in her for one
thing ...?'

Rachel heard the sting of Richard's hand across
Moira's cheek and her swift cry of pain.

'Get out.' His voice was low with fury. 'Get out!'

The door slammed and they heard a car rev and
drive away. A moment or two later the door opened
and closed again more quietly and they heard Richard
drive off.

Rachel looked at Ben. His face was ashen. 'It's not
true! Not Celia. Not my lovely Celia,' he muttered,
his voice almost a whisper.

'Didn't you know, Ben? Richard knew.'

He shook his head. 'I thought it was me she loved.
Not that we ever ... I mean, she was always faithful
to him ... at least, that's what I thought. That's why
I admired her so.' He sat on the bed and put his head
in his hands. After a long time he lifted his head. 'I
don't think I can stay here. Everywhere I go I can see
her. It'll be worse now, knowing what she really
was....' He went down the stairs and out of the house.
Rachel picked up the tools he had left strewn around
and put them away, locked up the cottage and left. It
showed the state of Ben's mind that he had taken the
truck, leaving her no option but to walk the three miles
back to Kilfinan House.

She didn't mind. She was glad of the opportunity to
sort out her thoughts. With Moira's revelation everything fell into place. It was understandable that Rose
had suspected it was Ben Celia was going to that night,

although Richard had—quite rightly—denied that this was likely. Rachel gave a little moan. Richard. She had even imagined that he might have engineered his wife's death. Poor Richard! Even he had never suspected David McLeod. But it all fitted in. David McLeod, rich in his own right and with the added attraction of the up-and-coming playwright image. From what Rachel had heard of Celia Duncan she would find such a combination irresistible. But David, it would seem, had played Celia at her own game and this time the tables were turned; Celia was the rejected one, probably for the first time in her life. So had it really been an accident on the Dunglevin Road or had she deliberately run her car off the road above the loch? That was something nobody would ever know.

Rachel looked at her watch. It was nearly two o'clock. She wondered how Melanie was enjoying school. She realised with surprise that she had scarcely given the little girl a thought since overhearing Moira's shattering disclosure. And that was another thing. David McLeod must have been the man Melanie had accompanied her mother to meet, and not Ben, as Rachel had assumed at the time, which would explain the child's odd behaviour the night the McLeods came to dinner; the way she had clung possessively to Rachel and refused to utter a word. And then her nightmare —'Don't go! Don't leave me!' She had simply been reliving the past. It was all there, if only they had known.

Rachel turned in at the drive and pulled her anorak more closely round her. She had enjoyed the walk, it had given her time to sort out her thoughts, but she was cold now and would be glad of a warming cup of tea before going to meet Melanie at half past three.

Suddenly she heard a motor coming towards her at breakneck speed. It was Ben, riding a motor-bike. She stepped aside in astonishment; she hadn't known he possessed such a vehicle; she had always seen him driving the truck, or, more occasionally, the Mini. He passed her without seeming to see her, his suitcases hurriedly strapped to the pillion. Poor Ben, she thought. Where would he go? What would he do? She hoped he would find happiness somewhere, but she doubted if she would ever see him again.

She continued up the drive and into the warm kitchen at Kilfinan House. Mrs Munroe had gone home and wouldn't be back until it was time to cook the evening meal, but she had left everything clean and neat. Rachel took off her anorak and hung it over a chair, then she made herself a pot of tea and sat down by the stove to drink it.

She was sitting there, her hands round the mug as if to draw extra warmth right down into the coldness that was inside her and nothing to do with the chillness of the day, when Richard came in.

'Would you like a cup of tea?' she asked, keeping her voice carefully polite.

'Thank you.' He leaned against the rail of the stove and watched her pour the amber liquid into a mug she had taken from a hook on the dresser.

'What's got into Ben?' he asked as she handed it to him. 'He's gone off on that old motor-bike of his as if all the devils in hell were after him.'

'I don't think he'll be coming back, either.' Rachel sat down and picked up her own mug without meeting his eyes.

Richard frowned at her. 'Have you quarrelled, then?'

'Good heavens, no!' She looked up in surprise. 'Nothing like that.'

'What then? My right-hand man—or, at least, my father's right-hand man, goes roaring off and you say he's not likely to be coming back. I think I'm owed some explanation as to why.'

Rachel studied the steam rising from her mug for some time without speaking.

'Ben and I were in the little bedroom at the head of the stairs at Arden Lodge, hanging curtains, when you and Moira came there this morning,' she said at last. 'We couldn't help overhearing your conversation. There was no way we could escape except by coming down the stairs, and that would have been even more embarrassing. I'm sorry, we couldn't help hearing.'

Richard was silent for a very long time, sipping his tea and staring into space. Rachel stole a glance at him. His jaw was set and stern and a small pulse was beating at his temple. She noticed a faint fleck of silver in his dark hair as he bent his head to his mug. She closed her eyes. It was no good, she knew that she would always love this man who had endured so much; an unfaithful wife, a disturbed daughter, the loss of the fishing business he was trying to build to assert his independence; and she admired the way he had taken on the running of his father's estate, an estate that was so run down that it would take all his skill and ingenuity to save it. There was still an angry scar on his hand to remind him of the day he lost his boat *Celia*, but apart from a stiffness in the fingers which made writing difficult that, at least, was back to normal. She wanted to put out her hand and touch the jagged red line that ran across his palm. Suddenly he looked very lonely and very vulnerable and her heart went out to him.

He put his mug down on the table and looked at her, his eyes puzzled. 'I can't understand why overhearing that conversation should have had such an effect on Ben,' he said.

'Because—didn't you know? Ben was in love with

Celia—or rather, with what he thought Celia was.'

Richard looked puzzled.

'In effect, Ben saw Celia as the beautiful princess married to a cold-hearted prince,' she explained. 'He saw himself as the humble woodman she fell in love with but was too high-principled to allow anything to come of it. He worshipped her from afar and imagined that she felt the same way about him.' She paused. 'You can imagine that the truth came as a blow. His idol was not only toppled from her pedestal but shattered into a thousand pieces.'

'You're exaggerating. Nobody could be that naïve in this day and age.'

'Maybe. I don't know much about Ben's background, except that he came from some remote island, but I've heard the way he spoke of Celia. I've seen the reverent way he treated the snapshot he had of her. And I saw his face as he heard what Moira said.... They say listeners hear no good of themselves, in this case it was even worse for Ben to hear no good of Celia.'

'So you knew how he felt about Celia?'

'Oh, yes, I've always known.'

He pulled her to her feet and still holding her, put his finger under her chin and made her look up at him. 'Poor little Rachel,' he said softly, 'and you came here to mend a broken heart. It hasn't been very successful, has it? Out of the frying pan into the fire would hardly be too strong a phrase, would it?'

He gazed at her, his eyes for once full of compassion. It was almost more than she could bear and her eyes filled with tears.

'We could try to find him.' He spoke slowly, almost reluctantly. 'It shouldn't be difficult, he can't have gone far. And I'm sure when he's had time to think, to get over the shock....'

She shook her head, unable to trust herself to speak. 'No,' she managed to get out at last, 'you don't understand. It's not ... Ben.'

How much more she would have confessed at that moment if the phone had not shrilled she was never quite sure. With Richard so close and so tenderly concerned it would have been easy—in fact, almost impossible not to put her head on his shoulder and tell him that Ben could go to Mars for all she cared as long as she could stay right there, where she was, encircled in Richard's arms.

But the phone rang, and Richard after a second's hesitation, when it seemed to Rachel that he held her just a shade closer, went to answer it.

She sat down weakly and searched for a tissue to blow her nose, trying to compose herself. She had come close to revealing her true feelings to Richard Duncan just then. It mustn't happen again. He had made it obvious that marriage—even a marriage of convenience to save the Estate—was not for him. It would only embarrass him to find out how she felt about him. The sooner she could leave Glencarrick the better it would be. She got up and picked up the mugs to take them to the sink and wash them up. She was running the water when Richard came back into the room, his face suddenly white and haggard.

'It's Melanie,' he said. 'She's run away from school. That was her headmaster. He says they've trained binoculars on the mountain and they think it's her they can see. It looks as if she's on her way home over the mountain track. She'll come to no harm as long as she keeps to the track and the mist doesn't come down.' He looked anxiously out of the window at the grey autumn afternoon. 'But I must say it doesn't look too healthy out there. Come on, we must go and fetch her.'

CHAPTER TWELVE

It didn't take Richard long to collect together what he needed to go after Melanie. By the time Rachel had donned boots and a thick sweater and anorak he was ready with compass, binoculars, whistle and rope.

'That mountain track is a short cut to Ardenbeg for people who know exactly what they're doing in the summer time, and even then it can be very tricky,' he explained, seeing her surprise at the precautions he was taking. 'Nobody in their right mind uses it at this time of year, especially late in the afternoon when the weather is threatening to close in as it is.' He looked at his watch. 'However, Melanie should be nearly home by now. If she isn't something must have gone wrong.'

Together they set off on the track to Ardenbeg. It was well-trodden and well-defined at first, almost wide enough for a car, although it was muddy from recent rain, but as they climbed higher it narrowed to a single footpath, which almost disappeared in places.

'If it's as bad as this the other side she'll never have followed it,' Richard said anxiously, 'and then goodness knows where she could have wandered to.'

'How long should it take her?' Rachel had to run a little to keep pace with his longer stride.

'Oh, I should say not much more than an hour, at the very most. They missed her at school around three o'clock ... let's see, allowing for her to have gone half an hour before that....' he looked at his watch. 'I should have thought she would have been in sight, at least.' He raised his binoculars and scanned the side of the mountain. 'But I can't see any sign of her. Here, you have a look.'

Rachel took the binoculars. The mountain looked cold and unfriendly, even the sheep huddling in clutches under the shelter of boulders. A wraith-like mist was beginning to curl itself thinly across the rugged contours. Rachel couldn't help contrasting this with the bright summery scene the first time she had walked the track to Ardenbeg, when Richard had rightly chastised her for her foolishness. She remembered, too, how quickly the whole mountain had been covered by the mist. No wonder Richard was worried!

He began to call, cupping his hands round his mouth. 'Melanie!'

They listened. There was no answer. In fact, the very silence seemed loud.

'If she's missed the track she could be anywhere.' Richard stopped and looked around. The mist was thickening—not suddenly as it had on the day they climbed to see Eas Mhor, the Great Waterfall, but slowly, insidiously, almost unnoticeably. The air was chill and there was a stillness over everything. For the hundredth time he looked at his watch. 'We should have picked her up by now. I didn't think there'd be any problem or I'd have alerted the rescue team.' He peered through his binoculars again. 'The fog's coming in thicker now.' He took a deep breath. 'Look, Rachel, do you think you can find your way back to the house? It's quite straightforward as the weather is now, you simply keep your eye on Kilfinan and keep going towards it, you can't go wrong. When you get there, call out the rescue team—the number's prominent by the telephone. I'll go on. Surely, she can't be far from here, but even a few yards off the track and we could miss her.' He cupped his hands again, 'Melanie!'

It was then that they heard it, faintly, in the distance. 'Daddy!'

'Melanie!' Richard called again.

'Daddy!'

Richard grabbed Rachel's hand. 'This way.' He raised his voice. 'Keep calling. Melanie. We're coming! We'll find you.'

Melanie's voice sounded nearer and nearer through the mist until at last they saw her, sitting huddled at the foot of a small scree.

'I fell. I've hurt my foot,' she whimpered as Richard scrambled down to her.

He picked her up bodily and carried her back to where Rachel was waiting. She put out her hand and Rachel took it.

'I'm not going to school any more, Rachel. I'm not going to leave you, not ever again.' Her face was tear-stained and grubby, but she smiled at Rachel and wouldn't relinquish her hand even on the awkward mountain slopes as Richard carried her down.

Once home Rachel bathed her and bandaged up her ankle. Then, as she sat in Rachel's sitting room in her fluffy pink dressing gown, drinking warm milk and eating a boiled egg, Richard gently questioned her.

'Didn't you like it at school today, little one?' he asked kindly.

'Oh, yes. We did lots of nice things and there were lots of children to play with. I liked it.'

'Then why did you run away?'

'Because of Rachel.'

'Because of me? Why?' Rachel asked, puzzled.

'Because I didn't want you to go away. And if I go to school you'll go away, I know you will. I heard Miss McLeod say so this morning.'

Rachel looked at Richard and he nodded. 'Moira came into Ardenbeg with us this morning and we were talking about school. Moira remarked. . . .'

'I see.' Rachel cut him short. She could just hear Moira saying, 'Now Melanie is at school you'll be able to get rid of her governess,' without Richard twisting the knife in the wound by actually repeating the words.

'So I came home.' Melanie beamed at them both. 'I'd have been home much sooner if I hadn't fallen and hurt my foot.' She looked at her bandaged ankle. 'Is it broken, Rachel?'

'No, you've just sprained it, that's all.' Rachel picked Melanie up off her chair and sat down herself with the little girl on her knee. 'But you mustn't run away like that, darling. Think what might have happened if we hadn't found you. You could have been there all night. Promise you won't run away from school again.'

'Oh, I won't run away again, because I'm not going. I'm going to stay at home with you.' Melanie smiled happily.

Rachel frowned. She didn't quite know what to say. She looked at Richard for guidance, but his expression gave no help.

Suddenly he got up and lifted his little daughter off Rachel's knee. 'I'm going to take you to bed, little one,' he said. 'You've had rather a nasty experience and you need a good night's rest.'

Melanie put out her hand. 'Rachel?' she asked. 'You're coming too?'

'No,' Richard said firmly, 'Rachel isn't coming too. I'm going to put you to bed. You rely far too much on Rachel, child.'

He was right, Rachel admitted to herself as she cleared Melanie's tea things away; Melanie had begun to rely too much on her. Perhaps the best thing to do would be to pack up and leave, before Alistair and Rose returned, so that Melanie would settle down at school and forget her. While she was here Melanie would never be any different. She went into her bedroom and dragged out a suitcase.

'Rachel! Rachel! Where are you?' Richard's voice called from the sitting room.

She brushed her hand across her face to try and compose herself and went to the door of the bedroom.

'Ah, there you are.' He came over to her and took her by the shoulders. 'Now,' he said, 'will you tell me once and for all what there is between you and Ben Carson'. He looked positively fierce as he waited for her answer.

'Nothing. Nothing at all.' She was too dazed by his tone to be other than completely truthful.

'And there's nobody else?'

'Like whom?' She was bewildered.

'David McLeod.... Oh, I don't know....'

Rachel shook her head wearily. 'No, there's nobody at all. Why do you ask?'

He let his hands slide down her arms till he could take her hands in his. 'Rachel, I know you said only this morning that you could never marry a man you didn't love, but do you think that perhaps, in certain circumstances, you just might?' His voice had lost its firmness, was almost humble. 'Do you think, for Melanie's sake, you could marry me, Rachel? She loves you so much and needs you so badly—almost, God help me, as much as I do.' He dropped her hands and turned away.

She caught her breath. 'Oh, Richard, do you really mean that?'

'Of course I mean it,' he said impatiently. 'Do you think I haven't gone through hell watching you with

Ben Carson? I've even tried to think of ways to get him sacked. And when I saw you coming out of Rose's bedroom with him....'

'Oh, Richard, I love you!'

He turned back to her, a look of absolute incredulity on his face. 'Say that again.'

'I love you, Richard.'

In an instant he gathered her into his arms and there was no holding back this time as his mouth came down on hers. A long time later Rachel smiled up at him. 'Just to set your mind at rest, Ben had only that minute come upstairs to see what was wrong when I slipped on the polished floor in Rose's bedroom.'

He groaned. 'My insane jealousy made far more of it than that. I went through hell!'

'Just as I did when I saw you kissing Moira the night she and David came to dinner.'

'That was an act of bravado, so that you shouldn't know how much I cared.'

'Oh, Richard, how stupid we've both been!'

'Not any more, though.' He began kissing her again.

'Shall we go and tell Melanie?' Rachel said when, much later, he paused for breath. 'I think she'll approve.'

'I know she will.' Richard kept her within the circle of his arm as they went across the corridor to Melanie's bedroom.

'Rachel's going to stay here for always, little one,' he whispered to his little daughter. 'She's going to marry me and be your mother.'

'Oh,' Melanie's voice was thick with sleep. 'That's good. That means I'll still be able to go to school. I didn't really want not to go. School was nice. But I couldn't lose Rachel. Now I can have both.' Her voice slurred. School and a new mummmmmy....' She drifted into sleep with a smile of utter contentment on her face.

There was much excitement over Rose and Alistair's homecoming. Richard and Rachel had secretly planned their wedding for the week after their return and Melanie was to be bridesmaid. As they broke the news over dinner on their first evening together Alistair turned to his wife and covered her hand with his own.

'We saw it coming, my love, didn't we? Right from the beginning.'

Rose nodded happily. 'Right from the beginning.'

Richard raised his eyes in mock exasperation. 'What did I tell you, Rachel? My father knows me almost better than I know myself. Well, Father, what else do you predict?'

'I never actually make predictions,' Alistair smiled. He raised his glass. 'But I hope that you will find as much happiness together as Rose and I have.'

'Amen to that,' said Rose.

And as Rachel looked at her aunt and saw the serene happiness in her face she realised that she could wish for nothing better.

And there's still *more* love in

Harlequin Presents...

Yes!

Six more spellbinding romantic stories every month by your favorite authors. Elegant and sophisticated tales of love and love's conflicts.

Let your imagination be swept away to exotic places in search of adventure, intrigue and romance. Get to know the warm, true-to-life characters. Share the special kind of miracle that love can be.

Don't miss out. Buy now and discover the world of HARLEQUIN PRESENTS...

Do you have a favorite
Harlequin author?
Then here is an
opportunity you must
not miss!